Franklin's Fate

BARRY DEANE STEWART

 www.trafford.com

North America & international
toll-free: 1 888 232 4444 (USA & Canada)
fax: 812 355 4082

READER ALERT

This novel, Franklin's Fate, is the third book in a series by the author. It is the continuation of the general story that unfolded in Drake's Dilemma and Vancouver's Vengeance. This book can be read on its own but it will divulge plot details of those previous books. The reader would undoubtedly enjoy those books more if they were read before this one.

Franklin's Fate

A Novel
Barry Deane Stewart

CONTENTS

Major Characters xv

Historical Event xvii

Book One   The Investigation 1

Book Two   The Dealer 23

Book Three   The Franklin Connection 41

Book Four   The Franklin Story 77

Book Five   The Pursuit 103

Book Six   The Renewal 155

Book Seven   The Surrounding 189

Epilogue 213

AUTHOR'S NOTES AND
ACKNOWLEDGEMENTS

This is a work of fiction. The story and characters are totally the imagination of the author. A few historical events are referenced in the text but are there to provide context only. They are not integral to the story.

In particular, this novel includes an abridged description of the voyages, adventures, and unfortunate fate of Sir John Franklin. Again I have endeavored to keep faith with the historical record, but there are necessarily some simplifications. The section that describes the last Franklin Expedition's experiences was totally created by the author, based on some artifacts that have been discovered, historical tales that have been related by the Inuit, and general knowledge about life in the British Navy in the 1800s. No manuscripts or diaries from the expedition have ever been found. Thus, please treat it as informed fiction.

This novel is a continuation of the story in my earlier *Drake's Dilemma* and *Vancouver's Vengeance*. All errors of fact, language, or style are mine. I have generally used modern American spelling, although there are a few obvious places where British or Canadian spelling was required.

I am a collector of antiquarian books and maps related to the exploration of the northern and western reaches of North America and I am an avid reader of that history. I am fortunate to have copies of many of the publications and maps referred to in this book in my own collection, which provided much of the research information for the story. I enjoy sharing my passion about the world of ancient explorers and their amazing journals and illustrations.

Drake's Dilemma described the adventures and exploits of Sir Francis Drake in the late 1500s. *Vancouver's Vengeance* moved the historical references two hundred years ahead to the 1700s, to the time of extensive exploration of the North Pacific. Now, *Franklin's Fate* has us experiencing Arctic exploration in the 1800s.

There have been many books written about Franklin and Arctic exploration in general. In writing this novel I have relied on a few of them, notably *The Arctic* Grail by Pierre Berton, The *Man Who Ate His Boots* by Anthony Brandt, *Across the Top of the World* by James Delgado and *The Search for the North West Passage* by Ann Savours. The Franklin story plus the description of the extensive efforts that were involved in finally locating the two long-lost ships of the Franklin Expedition are well captured in *Franklin's Lost Ship – The Historic Discovery of HMS Erebus* by John Geiger and Alanna Mitchell and *Sir John Franklin's Erebus and Terror Expedition – Lost and Found* by Gillian Hutchinson.

Other books that I reviewed include *Great Explorers* by Roderic Owen, *The Book of Exploration* by Ray Howgego and *A History of Polar Exploration* by David Mountfield.

The main storyline again occurs in the modern world of antiquarian book collecting. As before, I ask the experts to accept my generalities. My great thanks once more to the many outstanding people in the antiquarian books world who have guided my learning and the acquisition of my collection over the past years.

This book contains explanations of the history and inner workings of the rare book world, especially the relationships between major institutions, such as universities, libraries and foundations, and bookdealers and collectors. My knowledge had been overwhelmingly increased by the outstanding publication of speeches and papers by the late William Reese, *Collectors, Booksellers and Libraries: Essays on Americanists and the Rare Book Market*. Bill Reese was an unparalleled leader in the rare book world.

The issue of thievery of rare books and maps has had limited exposure. Some informative books about thefts of rare books and maps include *The Man Who Loved Books Too Much* by Allison Bartlett, *The Map Thief* by Michael Blanding, *The Island of Lost Maps* by Miles Harvey and *The Book Thief* by Travis McDade.

My wife Pat was once more the encouraging force that gave me the energy to write this third novel. Again she was the primary copyeditor and proofreader. The book is much better due to her input. I thank her very much.

Other friends and family members have also provided advice and encouragement. I thank them all, and in particular, my adult children, Deron, Deane and Heather, who reviewed my first draft and provided story suggestions.

Enjoy,

Barry Deane Stewart

Major Characters

Book Sellers:

Yrrab "Herb" Trawets	Pismo Beach, California
Andrew Dunlop	CARBCo Books, Philadelphia
Terrance Kent	Schuylkill River Books, Philadelphia
Alexander "Sasha" Rusti	Metro Rare Books, Philadelphia
Jeremy Boucher	Columbus, Ohio
Simon Katz	New York, New York
Margaret Thomas	Los Angeles, California

Law Enforcement:

Sybil Stella Stephens	Director, FBI
Efrem Z. Wilson	FBI, Washington
Mark Barnett	FBI, Washington
Leonard Nelson	FBI, Washington
Wilma Watkins	FBI, Washington
Karl Kolby	FBI, Philadelphia
Ernie Haas	FBI, Philadelphia

Woodbridge Heritage Institute:

Rhonda Wright	Director
Katherine Clay	Assistant Director
Dennis Davis	Curator
Emma Johnston	Book Restorer

Esposito Organization:

Antonio "Tony" Esposito	Boss
Hugo Cici	Senior Associate
Alberto Danza	Underling

Historical Event

In the summer of 2018 the antiquarian book world was shaken by the news of a major theft of rare antiquarian books from the Carnegie Library in Pittsburgh.

The curator of the Rare Books Collection had stolen over 300 valuable books from the collection over two decades. It had gone undetected until a routine insurance audit uncovered the gaps in the collection. The curator had been the sole person responsible for the acquisition and management of the books. There had been no organizational oversight.

The curator had supplied the books to an established rare book dealer in Pittsburgh, who then sold the books into the market via book fairs and online listings.

The books had a retail value of over eight million dollars. Very few of the books have been recovered.

BOOK ONE

The Investigation

1

It was February and Herb Trawets was just finishing his mid-morning coffee.

The doorbell rang. Opening the door, he saw a fortyish man dressed in a business suit with a white shirt and necktie, somewhat of an anomaly in his relatively casual retirement neighborhood. He was carrying a small folio briefcase.

"Mr. Trawets?" he asked.

"Yes."

"I am Agent Efrem Wilson with the FBI. I called you earlier. May I come in?"

"Certainly."

After they were seated in Herb's living room, Herb asked, "What is this concerning?"

"Well, Mr. Trawets, as I briefly stated on the phone, I am investigating a number of facets of the antiquarian book business and I was hoping you could help me.

"How did you find me?" Herb asked, with an unintended double meaning.

"I know that you have dealt extensively with President Cartwright regarding his collection of rare books. My investigation has involved him and he recommended you as someone who is very knowledgeable and discreet, and who might be able to give me some new ideas."

"Well, I would be pleased to help you in any way that I can. Tell me more."

"It's a bit complicated, but I'm investigating the robbery and forgery of antiquarian documents and possible links to money laundering activities. I need some help."

Herb sat calmly, gathering himself for what might follow next. Ever since Agent Wilson had called an hour earlier asking to meet him, he had speculated about what was going to happen. After all, he had forged an ancient document attributed to Sir Francis Drake; he had sold it to President Cartwright for $2.5 million through a maze of camouflaging actions; he had secured the funds for himself via a complicated financial transaction that involved a cousin's international money transfer business; and he had tried to sell a second copy of the fake document to a wealthy California book collector, Louis Wing. Forgery. Money laundering. Was the FBI on his trail?

2

"Well, Mr. Trawets, it all started with a document that President Cartwright purchased a number of years ago. You will likely recall the time as you were involved with the payment for the document."

"I recall his purchasing a document, supposedly related to Sir Francis Drake, which required him to make an international payment. I helped him to arrange financing and I did transfer the funds, but that was about all. In reality, it was a very strange process in that President Cartwright asked me a lot of general questions but he never showed me the document he was buying. I had worked with him in creating his large book collection over many years and nothing like that had happened before. Of course I didn't pursue it very much as he was such an important client; he was actually Vice President then."

"Yes, he explained all that to me."

"Then, what is the issue?"

"Let me show you the document and ask you to give me your opinion of it."

With that, Wilson reached into his briefcase and extracted a small document. It was just four old-looking pages, bound together with leather ties and covered in old fashioned printing. He handed it to Herb.

"Is this what President Cartwright bought?" asked Herb.

"Yes. Read it and tell me what you think."

Herb took the document and read through it thoroughly. Being eight sides of old print, that took him over fifteen minutes. Of course, he had to pause and think for moments, re-read some parts, and appear totally focused. Mostly he was composing his response, since he knew the content well. He had written it.

"Well," he said. "That is certainly an amazing and historic document, if it's real."

"Do you think it's real?"

"I don't know, but I would be somewhat skeptical."

"Why?"

Herb laughed in a low tone. "Well, to start with I have just been handed it by an FBI agent who says he is investigating forgery of documents."

"What else?"

"I would want to read it more thoroughly and ask many questions, but my first reaction was one of doubt, as I said. When you analyze a document for authenticity, you approach it in three general ways: content, technical details, and context.

"Content is obvious but is the least meaningful. This tale by Drake is quite consistent with some recent research on his travels, although it is quite different than the historic record. But that doesn't mean much. A fake document can contain true information.

"Technical details for antiquarian documents include an analysis of the paper, the ink, the type set, the bindings, etc. After all, the document is supposed to be from 1595, over 425 years ago. I assume that has been done?"

"Yes," Wilson replied. "It was inconclusive."

"What is also unusual is that it is four loose pages bound together with leather ties. That's not impossible, but very unlikely.

"Context is the third dimension. Here, I would need to do some more detailed research about Drake and his times, but there are unusual things. It is supposedly a very secret document, even for those times, and yet it is printed, not handwritten. Why? Printing was very controlled in those days.

"Also, a printed document implies more than one copy. Why hasn't a copy, or even a rumor of such a document, appeared in over four hundred years?

"As I said, all-in-all I would doubt its authenticity. Did President Cartwright really buy this for all that money we transferred?"

"Yes, and he now knows it is a fake."

"Oh! Why-oh-why didn't he confide in me or some other expert. I guess even people as smart as President Cartwright can get caught up with Collector's Disease, the irresistible urge to own something that no one else has."

Wilson just smiled with a slight grimace.

"The second thing I wanted to ask you about was the transfer of the funds to pay for the document."

Herb paused for a minute, gathering his thoughts. He didn't know if Wilson knew anything about the fundraising methods that Cartwright had used to get the funds. He didn't think any of the actions to buy books on a delayed basis and to divert funds to an alternative purchase were illegal; after all it was all Cartwright's money and books. He decided to keep it simple and see what unfolded.

"The payment was straightforward. I received a check from the administrator of his trusts. I sent some of the money to a couple of dealers, including myself, for various activities we had done, and the bulk of the funds, over two million dollars I recall, to a numbered bank account in the Bahamas."

"What did you know about that account?"

"Nothing. It was just a number that President Cartwright gave me."

"OK, thanks. You have reinforced everything else we were able to determine about the transaction."

"Fine. Is that all?"

"No, actually that was just me cleaning up some loose ends around that investigation. My main purpose in coming to see you is a totally different topic."

3

"Oh," said Herb, with a bit of a surprised look and a slight sigh of relief that he hoped Wilson didn't notice.

"It has to do with book thieves and money laundering."

"Book thieves?"

"Yes, can you give me your general sense of the issue in your business?"

"Books do get stolen. If you have a retail store, pilfering is possible, as it is in any business. Staff working in bookstores can easily take books. Inventory in bookstores is usually very large, consists of relatively small items and is often somewhat disorganized. Inventory taking is almost never done; it would be a prohibitive undertaking."

"What about robbery on a larger scale?"

"I don't know that I've heard about large-scale robberies of books. Unlike famous pieces of art that are worth millions of dollars and inspire elaborate schemes to steal them from major institutions such as the Louvre, boxes of books are bulky and heavy, and individual items aren't in the same class as a Rembrandt. Also, reselling books is not an easy proposition. If they are valuable books, it's hard to get good prices if you don't have a reputation and a good customer base."

"Haven't there been some famous episodes?"

"Oh sure, episodes but not epidemics as far as I know. There was one fellow that stole books by using fake or stolen credit cards. He was stealing for his own collection, not to resell them for a profit. That story was written in a popular book, *The Man Who Loved Books Too Much.* There have also been a few famous cases of people cutting maps and illustrations out of books in libraries and such for resale. Those types of items are easier to sell."

"What about the books stolen from the Carnegie Library in Pittsburgh?"

"Now, that was something else altogether. I don't know all of the details but what was reported was quite startling."

"Tell me your interpretation of what happened."

"As reported, the curator of the rare book collection at the Carnegie removed about three hundred valuable books from the collection over perhaps two decades and provided them to an antiquarian book dealer who sold them into the market. The books were valued at over eight million dollars. The theft was only discovered when an inventory audit was done for insurance purposes."

"How could the theft have gone undetected for so long?"

"Actually, it was a bit of an unusual event that detected it. Library audits for insurance purposes are not often done. Invoices and records are usually adequate."

"But, it's a library. What happened when someone wanted to see a book that was missing?"

"It's a sad state of affairs for major collections of rare books today; they are seldom accessed. Since the 90's essentially every book has been digitized. Researchers don't need to travel afar to various libraries to see the information.

The net effect is that many libraries are no longer adding to their collections, except perhaps in a few very specific areas of interest. Budgets for universities allocate funds to other priorities.

"That also applies to staffing levels. At the Carnegie, the curator was the only person involved with the special collections for the last few decades. He did the purchasing, record keeping, maintenance, etc., etc. with no oversight by anyone else.

"Apparently the curator even took some actions and made a list of things he could say if someone did happen to inquire about a missing book. For example, he created a list of some of the missing books but also included books that were still there on the list. Then he would add later notes, saying those books had been found, having been misfiled on the shelves. This would create the impression that a missing book was probably there in some incorrect place. He could also claim that a book was out on loan or was out for repairs.

"In addition, he would leave his special area unattended and unlocked for extended periods, so that he could claim that someone could have entered the area and removed some books.

"But, in reality, no one ever noticed the missing books."

"That's amazing," said Wilson. "Then, what happened to the stolen books?"

"Well, as I said, he supplied them to a local book dealer who sold them at book fairs, at auctions and online."

"Didn't the dealer need to explain where he got the books?"

"Not really. He was a reputable dealer and he could just say it came from a family estate, or another dealer, or a local auction in England, or whatever. In fact many books do come into the market from old family collections, driven by the three-Ds of debt, divorce and death. That's often accompanied by a desire to keep the disposal private.

"Also it's not unusual for dealers to keep their sources confidential to prevent other dealers from preempting them in the future. Most buyers don't pay a lot of attention to a book's provenance unless it's something special or involves somebody extra important. Even rare books can have many copies in existence. Unless there are some special markings they can all look alike. Books can be cleaned, rebound and even trimmed to alter their appearance without affecting value."

"So, these two people, working in tandem, were able to steal three hundred books and sell them for eight million dollars."

"No, not even close. As reported in the press, the curator received about one thousand dollars per book, or a total of about three hundred thousand dollars."

"That's all?"

"Yes, apparently he needed extra money to supplement his librarian salary but that was sufficient. Also, he had no way to sell the books directly himself."

"So the dealer made the big profit?"

"More so than the curator but not necessarily huge amounts. There was an example given in the same press reports that described the trail of one book that has been recovered. The curator got his one thousand dollars. The dealer sold the book to another dealer at a book fair for five thousand dollars. That dealer later sold the book for thirty-five thousand dollars to a group of three other dealers who advertised it online for ninety-five thousand dollars. The only reason this came to light was that it all happened relatively late in the scheme of things and it was a book with very special provenance. The book was a rare French treatise on the economics of trade between France and the United States, inscribed by President Jefferson. When the Carnegie authorities discovered their problem they tried to trace the various books, but had limited success. However, they did spot this one very identifiable one at the online site and were able to recover it. The dealers were out of luck, and out of pocket."

"Why would the curator take one thousand dollars and the dealer take five thousand dollars for a book that was going to end up in the market for almost one-hundred thousand dollars?"

"To start with, most of the books were not as valuable as that. They averaged about $25,000 per book. It takes time, sometimes years, and a network of contacts to find a buyer for very expensive books. It has been said that there is no such thing as a million dollar book, just a million dollar customer; someone who badly wants that specific item for their collection. The dealer who was involved with the theft didn't have those connections. It's quite common for a valuable book to move through a chain of dealers."

"Do you think this type of theft has happened at other institutions?"

"I don't know. Most people I've talked to tend to assume it was a unique event. I know libraries have been advised to check their collections but I really wonder how much has really been done. Major libraries can have tens of thousands of books, meaning it is a daunting task to take inventory. It would take a lot of staff time and money, neither of which are in large supply at those places. I suspect most have just reviewed and possibly revised their policies and procedures for managing valuable items. Also, the Carnegie situation where one individual had total control over the operation of their special collections may be unusual."

Herb Trawets and Agent Wilson continued to talk for another hour as Herb described in more detail the characteristics and processes that bookdealers, institutional curators and general collectors tended to exhibit. Wilson had picked up a general knowledge of all that when he was investigating the fake document that President Cartwright had bought and the subsequent unsuccessful sting operation to try to draw out the culprit, but Herb certainly added a lot of detail to his understanding.

As he was leaving, Agent Wilson said, "Thank you so much for taking all this time to talk with me. It has been very helpful. As I said earlier, we're investigating the possibility of a larger theft and money-laundering operation and I needed to get a better understanding of your trade. After President Cartwright mentioned your discretion, and that you were now retired from the business, it seemed ideal to contact you. I didn't want to contact anyone still active in the business, in order to maintain confidentiality about our investigation. You never know who might be involved. I trust you will keep this conversation private."

"Certainly," said Herb. "Contact me anytime if you want anything else."

"Will do. Thanks again."

After Agent Wilson departed, Herb let out a big sigh, feeling like it was the first time he had actually relaxed since earlier that morning when Wilson had called to arrange the meeting.

"Well, well," he thought. "Now I am sort of an insider into the investigations of fake and stolen books. How ironic."

Franklin's Fate

He also felt a great sense of comfort and satisfaction for his decision to abandon the sale of a second copy of the fake Sir Francis Drake document. When Wilson had shown him the Drake document, he had noticed a small smudge in the printing at the bottom of the second page. That was the copy he had tried to sell Louis Wing, not the one he had sold President Cartwright, in spite of what Wilson had said. So, the whole approach by Alan Page to get a second copy for Louis Wing had been a set-up after all. He had barely escaped detection back then. Thank goodness for his sixth sense.

4

Efrem Wilson flew back to Washington and met with the Director of the FBI, Sybil Stella Stephens.

"Director," said Wilson, "I had a very informative meeting with Herb Trawets in California but I didn't learn a lot new that will help us. He seemed genuinely surprised to see what President Cartwright had bought and his first reaction was one of doubt as to its authenticity, just as we heard from Jeremy Boucher when we first started the investigation. He even added the point that for Drake to have something like that printed, rather than just write it out was strange. As the President told us, he didn't seem to have any awareness of the involvement of Alan Page, the dealer who facilitated the whole con."

"What about the book thievery activities?"

"Trawets certainly knew about the Carnegie robbery and it was apparent that it had been the subject of discussion in the book dealer world. However, he tended to brush it off as a unique, outlying event, not a part of any larger scheme.

"He did give me a lot of background on how the bookselling world works. It's apparent that a knowledgeable person, probably a dealer, could easily dispose of stolen books if he used secondary book fairs, regional auctions, and online listings, as long as the books didn't have some unique identification and he was willing to sell for well below full collector value to insert them into the chain of dealers and customers."

"Well, I know that's consistent with what we have heard from some others, including some of the Directors of large libraries and museums, but it still doesn't ring true to me," said Stephens. "When we conducted the investigation into the fake document that President Cartwright bought, I was surprised at how easily the two-plus million dollar payment disappeared into the international banking system; that sure felt like it was part of a larger money laundering organization.

"Then when we investigated the Carnegie robbery, I was amazed that the two main culprits gained so little. Out of a set of books that was supposedly worth eight million dollars, the thief got about three hundred thousand and the primary dealer maybe five times that or so. Someone else has gained over six million dollars. How can that be? And how can that be a one-off event?"

"We are hearing from many people that it's all quite possible."

"Many of those people have reasons to want to believe that. If there is a wider spread thievery and money laundering activity going on it will make many senior people in a large number of high-profile organizations look totally foolish and incompetent. Maybe even leave them vulnerable to legal action or lawsuits challenging their handling of their governance responsibilities and fiduciary duties. Remember the scandals involving ancient Greek and Roman antiquities a few years ago; people went to jail."

"Director, what do you want us to do?"

"I don't want to let this disappear into the archives without additional investigation. There could be millions of dollars of thefts involved, large-scale money laundering, and who knows about illegal payments and kick-backs in public institutions."

"We don't have any real leads and it could take a lot of resources to find any," pushed back Wilson, gently.

"I accept that. Start with a small team and try to identify the most likely places that this problem could be happening and start there. If it all ends up in a dead end after a reasonable effort, then I will call it all off unless something else more tangible surfaces to restart our activities."

"OK, will do," said Wilson.

5

Returning to his office Wilson gathered a few of his associates together. They had worked together on various fraud, extortion and financial investigations over the past number of years.

They were Agent Mark Barnett, who specialized in monetary and financial issues; Agent Leonard Nelson, who specialized in data systems and internet activities; and Agent Wilma Watkins, who specialized in the world of art and antiquities.

He laid out the background for them.

"Oh boy," said Len Nelson, "It's not as if we're looking for a needle in a haystack; we're going to need to find the haystack first."

Mark Barnett said, "It seems you pursued the money transfers for the fake documents pretty thoroughly, and you don't seem to have any leads of fake sales and money flow related to the stolen Carnegie books. There's nowhere to start looking for an illegitimate money flow."

Wilma Watkins sat quietly through the early discussion. Then she asked, "How can we find a fresher trail of other stolen books, if they exist?"

"Well that would be a first," said Wilson. "We can call on people and say we're from the FBI and we wondered if we can check to see if anything was stolen from you. As opposed to every other situation where people call the FBI and report something stolen. But, let's give it a go for a while. If nothing surfaces after a reasonable time, I will just tell the Director that we are at a dead end."

Wilma said, "There are hundreds, even thousands of libraries and museums in the country. Where do we start?"

"Was there anything unusual or distinctive about the books that were stolen from the Carnegie library?" asked Mark.

"I don't know," answered Wilson. "Herb Trawets said they tried to trace the missing books and so they must have a list. I'm sure we can find it."

"Actually, I just found it," said Len, the systems expert who had a laptop computer in front of him. "I just searched for 'stolen books from Carnegie library' and it was there."

"Let me see," asked Wilma.

After a few minutes of scanning the lists, she said, "Well, we should have an expert look at this and give us a professional opinion but I can observe a few things. The books cover a wide range of topics: history, science, nature, exploration, philosophy, finance, etc., but don't seem to include literature. Many of the authors are very famous: Adams, Burke, Cook, Lincoln, Luther, Newton, Priestley, Raleigh, Smith, Washington, and so on. The books are listed alphabetically by author. They would appear to be famous, valuable and collectible, quite obvious targets for thieves. But that doesn't really tell us much."

"I'll send the list to Herb Trawets and ask him if he can decipher any deeper trends, but I agree that it's unlikely," said Wilson.

"Let's start by interviewing senior people at some major libraries to see if we can learn anything more about this issue. Wilma, perhaps you could make a list of ten or twelve places for us. Keep them to the northeast area for now; we don't need to undertake extensive travel at this stage."

6

Over the next number of weeks Agents Efrem Wilson and Wilma Watkins visited with eight organizations, including the heads of the New York Public Library, The Boston Library, The Smithsonian, the Woodbridge Heritage Institute, and the libraries at Harvard, Yale and NYU. The visits were spread over time as the agents had other cases they were working on and this one wasn't especially time sensitive, other than the Director had initiated it.

They stopped after eight visits because they were all tending to provide the same information.

The team regrouped in the Washington office and Wilma gave them a summary of their findings.

"We have learned a great deal about the workings of libraries and major institutions, but it really was just an elaboration on the general knowledge that Agent Wilson got from Herb Trawets.

"First of all, almost without exception, the leaders believe that the Carnegie situation was unusual and unique and they doubted that they had similar large-scale problems. They believed they had better security and oversight than Carnegie had. We couldn't test that.

"They acknowledged that they undoubtedly lose some books over time but have never detected a larger problem. We got the sense that some of the people we talked to didn't want there to be a problem. It would reflect on their organization's competence and reputation, and could impact support from donors and benefactors.

"Some said that taking a total inventory of their holdings was near impossible. Some have hundreds of thousands of book, some more. It would take an army of people and entail huge expenses to do a total inventory. They do not have those resources. A few had done a random sample inventory check after the Carnegie story broke and they said the number of missing books was small and some of that was likely due to errors in filing, sloppy records of withdrawals or books out for repair, and so on; the same excuses the Carnegie thieves had prepared if they were challenged. They just didn't think there was a real problem.

"Some of them did expand on our discussions to talk about the theft of rare maps, which has been an issue in the past. Apparently rare old maps are just as collectible as rare books. They also have a special place in history as they conveyed the latest knowledge of geography as the world was being explored from the middle ages through the 1800s. They were often treated as national secrets, for military, exploration and trade reasons. For example, we were told that it was a crime punishable by death to make any unauthorized copy of world maps in Portugal in the 15th and 16th centuries. Portugal was a world power in those days, as reflected even today in the Portuguese speaking areas of the East Indies, Southeast Asia, and Brazil.

"It turns out that many, if not most, of the rare maps from the 15th to 18th centuries were printed in books, either as atlases or as illustrations in the publications of explorers and traders. In order to get copies of individual maps for sale to collectors, books are often broken up as the parts can be worth much more than the whole in the marketplace.

"Almost all of the organizations we talked to have been victimized by maps being stolen from their books. The normal technique is for an individual to represent themselves as a researcher or dealer, or even a major collector, who is doing research in a particular area. Then, after getting a number of rare books to peruse at some desk or kiosk in the place, they use a razor blade to slice out specific maps when no one is looking. Maps are much easier to conceal than books and it would be unusual for anyone to check a book for a missing map when it was returned to the staff. An atlas can have dozens, even hundreds of maps.

"There were two very famous cases where an individual stole many maps from many institutions, including many of the ones we talked to. In 1995 a fellow named Gilbert Bland was apprehended; he had stolen over 250 maps. Ten years later, a guy named Forbes Smiley stole over 100 maps. They were worth millions. They were both caught due to a slip-up. They were caught in the act of stealing a map at a major library.

"The leaders we talked to were quite aggravated that the culprits were given rather light sentences. Directly to us they expressed the opinion that law enforcement officials don't treat the theft of books and maps very seriously. Our visit to them about possible stolen books didn't seem to impress them much; that had nothing to do with the lenient penalties in their opinions.

"One thing they did say was that once many of the maps were recovered they were able to identify some that were taken from their specific organization. The reason they could do that was because they could narrow down their search of their books to the ones the culprits had looked at. They had to register at the library to see the books.

"This did lead a couple of them to say to us that if we knew the name of a thief, or even if we could identify specific books that they stole, they could perhaps find a clue in their records of visitors and books inspected in their rare books area. Again they emphasized that they were not aware of any major book thefts, and pointed out it's much more difficult to take and not return a book, as compared to a map that has been removed from a book."

"Thanks, Wilma," said Wilson. "I think that summarizes our visits with the libraries very well. Any questions?"

Len spoke up first. "I'm sure I'll have lots of questions about details but, it seems to me, you're saying that you didn't uncover any leads, not even a significant concern about such thefts. Is that right?"

"I'm afraid it is," replied Wilson.

"Were there any discussions of the money dimensions of the book world?" asked Mark.

"Not much. These people just focus on getting budgets approved for acquisitions and on soliciting donations of funds or actual book collections from benefactors," answered Wilson.

"However," added Wilma, "a few did mention that their role as the collector of rare books was being questioned more and more by their organizations and supporters. There is some pressure on them to specialize. Many rare books are duplicated in many institutions and there are few people accessing them since the content is now usually available digitally. In the future they may be sellers as much as buyers of rare books."

"That leads nicely into the second part of our report," said Wilson. "When we were in New York we also visited with a major book dealer, Simon Katz. He's a much larger dealer than Herb Trawets was and he was also mentioned by President Cartwright as someone he very much trusted. Although we're trying to limit the knowledge of our investigation, I decided it was worth the risk to get a second opinion from him."

7

"As with the libraries, most of what we heard from Simon Katz was totally consistent with Herb Trawets, but he added a broader perspective," Wilson continued. "He didn't add any more details about the Carnegie theft itself, but did elaborate on some of the disposal activities.

"He emphasized that the book dealer world is very competitive, that unique finds were harder and harder to discover, and that margins were getting tighter, all due to the arrival of the internet and many online bookselling sites. He confirmed Trawets' observations that dealers tended to keep their sources confidential and even tried to shield their main customers. That's what leads to a given book moving through various dealer levels before finding an eventual home with a collector.

"For many collectors of rare books it's a hobby and often a show of wealth. He referred to the book collection on display in the movie *The Great Gatsby*, apparently all for show.

"Some collectors may have a special area of interest but they don't have the time to do detailed research. That's where a very knowledgeable dealer comes in. He both educates the customer and finds the books to fill the collection.

"Thus, he put the Jefferson book that was stolen from Carnegie in context. It was a little unusual for the crooked dealer to sell the valuable book for only $5000, but not unheard of; the second dealer would just presume he had a better sense of its real value and had a good deal. Selling it to the next dealer for $35,000 was a great profit and moved the book up the chain. Even then, the third dealer shared it with two other dealers to split the cost and increase their chance of selling it. They obviously didn't have a ready customer. Listing the book for sale at $95,000 was their way to test the market. They would likely have been willing to sell it for a 20% discount which is often given to other dealers and major customers. Thus the three dealers might realize $75,000, for a profit of $40,000 split three-ways. That might take quite a while to realize, with the inherent risk it might not sell for that much, and having tied up their money. Katz saw the process as being quite normal."

Mark Barnett, the finance expert, interjected. "That rings true to me. Time is money and it represents risk. Dead inventory is death in any business."

Wilson continued, "Katz also elaborated on the role of institutions in the rare book world. He started by using a quote from some past famous dealer named Warmser to the effect that "Rare books are becoming scarce!" On the surface that sounded like a silly gratuitous comment but Katz explained that it was said in frustration over the role of the institutions.

"He explained that for probably fifty years, from the Second World War until the 1990's, major collections of rare and historic books were created at many universities and special institutions. They preserved the books and made them available to historians and researchers. They dominated the market. In some famous instances, every known issue of a given book was locked away in the institutions; dealers and collectors could never hope to find one. They were frustrated that institutions could justify holding a fortune in little-used, duplicative collections.

"He also said some of the same things that Trawets and the librarians said, namely that the role is changing with the digital availability now. However, the books still dominantly reside in the institutions, even if they're not accessed often. Thus, the temptation to steal rare books exists, as the Carnegie case showed.

"Katz agreed that he didn't have any awareness of other large-scale thefts, but he was also skeptical that they would be easily detected. He, somewhat whimsically, said most thefts of rare books are probably done by family members in old estates with large libraries that no one visits, who then sell them to some local book dealer in confidence.

"He agreed that stolen books could be placed into the market by a knowledgeable person who knew the business, was patient, and was working at the lower levels if he was willing to take lower value, as was done with the Carnegie dealer. Provenance quickly gets lost in a chain of ownership. He even quoted a famous European, Goldschmidt, who said that every truly great book has been stolen at least twice, although he was generally referring to upheavals that come with wars or events like the French Revolution and the Russian Revolution.

"Finally, Katz also philosophized about rare books and their place today. As he summarized it, antiquarian books are both founts of knowledge and objects of beauty and collectability.

"The institutions who have dominated the market for so long are almost totally focused on preserving the knowledge they contain. That's why it's surprising to see that many books in the institutions are in poor shape. They don't care. Often the quality ones they have are either very special or have been part of collections donated by sponsors or alumni.

"Collectors, on the other hand, start with some interest in a subject and want a valuable collection. They find that books, with their inherent information and historical context, are more exciting than stamps or baseball cards. These collectors tend to just collect the major books related to their given subject, often those found in published lists of the most important fifty or hundred books for a topic, although some collectors do get deeper into their subject and then pursue secondary items, alternative printings and related ephemera.

"However, Katz concludes, there is an ever-increasing number of collectors and a limited number of books, and so there is a buyers' pressure on the market. Thus sellers who can secure new supplies will have good opportunities for profit, and be able to fight off the pressures that have caused many bookstores and booksellers to go out of business."

"So," said Len, "it's a thief's market."

"Did Katz have any thoughts on financial shenanigans such as money laundering?" asked Mark.

Wilma responded. "I tested him slightly about that but he didn't know of anything. When I used the term money laundering, he looked confused. He asked how could that fit in a chain of buying and selling transactions, with each step involving different people. I let the subject drop."

"Well," said Wilson, summarizing the meeting. "I think the word 'drop' is probably the operational one. We have learned a great deal about the antiquarian book business and the potential for theft, but we really haven't unearthed any real evidence of a crime and I don't think we have any other leads. I will tell the Director that we are putting everything on hold until and unless something more tangible surfaces. She won't be happy."

BOOK TWO

The Dealer

8

The dealer was sitting in his office, deep in thought.

"Is it time to change things? Maybe slow down? Shut down?" he wondered.

It had been a great ride for well over ten years. He had made millions of dollars and had never had any serious feeling of risk or detection. After all, he kept his public profile very professional. His other activities were done with low visibility, and the people he dealt with had an unyielding mantra of keeping secrets and staying silent.

Now, things had become more uncertain. All because of those two dolts who stole three hundred books from the Carnegie Library and got caught. Now the FBI was snooping around.

His name was Alexander Rusti, but everyone called him Sasha since that's what his mother always called him and his early friends picked up on it. He lived in Philadelphia.

He had started slowly in the business, over thirty years ago. Originally he opened a used book store, under the retail name Bye Buy Books. However, he realized after a few years that buying used books for five dollars and selling them for ten or twenty didn't end up netting much. You needed large inventory, which took a large space with commensurate rent, utilities, insurance, and staff costs. No matter how carefully you bought used books from the multitude of people who came in to sell books every day, you always ended up with too many books that didn't sell; just dead money. Bank loans accumulated. No wonder used book stores were closing down in a steady stream everywhere. Now, people could buy those ten dollar books online for seven dollars and have them delivered.

Then he encountered another dealer in the city who sold older books. His name was Ernest Markham. He called his books rare and antiquarian. They became friends over time, having lunches and happy-hour drinks together. He realized that there was more potential in that end of the business, but it seemed more complicated and involved investing higher amounts. Ernest gradually educated him in many of the intricacies – the need to be extra careful in buying; the need to cultivate customers as individuals, not as strangers; the need to really know your books of interest. Completeness, condition, rarity and marketability were paramount.

He tried to shape his own business in that direction but it was impossible; the two concepts were incompatible. Cheap books didn't justify all that attention.

Then he approached Ernest about joining him. After a number of discussions it was agreed that he could buy into the business and acquire it over time. It had the rather simple name Metro Rare Books. Ernest intended to retire in ten years and they worked out a plan for a purchase and ongoing royalties on future sales. The down payment came from selling his traditional used bookstore.

The next ten years were a whirlwind of activity. The business grew substantially as they moved their focus to higher value books and developed a growing network of customers. He learned steadily under the tutelage of his older partner and with the experiences of attending regional antiquarian book fairs and auctions.

However, there was a nagging issue. Even though he was expanding the business, selling more expensive books, and increasing the revenue, he wasn't realizing any large profit. Costs were high, competition for buying good books was significant, and thus margins were small. Inventory always represented a large sunk cost which was burdened by bank loans and lines of credit. He was feeling frustrated.

Things had started to change when he met Hugo Cici. He remembered when he first met Hugo and their early dealings well.

9

Sasha Rusti was sitting in his local pub, The Heath and Heather, a typical community establishment, complete with a long bar, free-standing tables, and booths along the walls, all highlighted by dark wood panels. It was faux English, just like the name.

It was early on a Friday evening and the place was relatively busy, with many of the customers stopping in after work for a drink before heading home for the weekend.

He was alone, as was usual. He didn't often drop by on Fridays, and he watched the dynamics of the larger-than-normal crowd before him absentmindedly as he sipped his gin martini. One large fellow caught his attention. He was dressed somewhat casually, with a sports jacket over an open-necked shirt and dark pants. He seemed to be moving from table to table, briefly talking to each group, making notes in a small notebook. Sometimes he could hear someone address the fellow as 'Big.'

As he passed the corner table where Sasha had settled, he raised an eyebrow in a questioning gesture. Sasha didn't understand and frowned. The fellow just smiled and said, "Fancy a wager on the weekend games?"

Sasha shook his head and smiled back a little sheepishly for some unknown reason.

After the now-obvious bookmaker finished his pass around the pub, he settled in at a newly-vacant table beside Sasha. After ordering a beer, he flipped through his notepad, adding a notation here and there. Finally he settled back and looked up. He saw Sasha looking at him and, again with a slight smile, said, "Hi, I'm Hugo Cici, although most people just call me Big." It was clearly a play on his name and his size.

The tables were close together and the two of them carried on an easy conversation, sticking to the generalities of sports, the weather and local news. During the dialogue Sasha mentioned his rare book business. After finishing his beer, Hugo Cici left quietly.

For some reason, maybe curiosity, Sasha turned up fairly regularly on Friday evenings after that and fell into a pattern of watching Hugo make his inevitable rounds. They even fell into the habit of chatting afterwards, now at his table. It wasn't clear why they did that; it just seemed to happen naturally.

Then, something new happened. Hugo Cici walked into Metro Rare Books one Monday morning.

10

Sasha looked up from behind a display counter and, with a bit of a surprised look, said, "Hi, Hugo. Welcome to my shop. It's good to see you. Are you interested in rare books? We haven't talked about it that much."

"Hi," Hugo responded. "I was more intrigued by the various things you mentioned during our conversations about how your business of buying and selling books worked and how some old books can be worth a lot of money."

"Sure," said Sasha, a bit puzzled. "How can I help?"

Hugo replied in a very careful, measured tone. "I was thinking that I could invest in rare books with your help."

Sasha suddenly had a slight tremor of uncertainty. Had he stumbled into a gangster world and was he about to be extorted? He knew those things happened to many small businesses. "In what way?" he said slightly stammering.

""In a very positive way. I would need your help to figure out the details, but let me show you what I was thinking. Have you got a very expensive book to show me that I can use as an example?"

Somewhat reluctantly he went to a glass-enclosed case and extracted a book. He said, "This is a book related to the early discoveries in Western Canada. It's called *The Wanderings of an Artist among the Indians of North America* by Paul Kane. It has a map and many impressive illustrations. It's for sale for $10,000. It is one of my best items."

"Perfect," said Hugo. "Now, what if I can buy it for $2000 and sell it back to you for $9,000 and I give you a $1,000 gratuity?"

"What! That makes no sense. I would lose $6,000. Why would I do that?"

"I left out the detail that when I buy the book I actually give you $10,000." Hugo expanded, "Think about what transpires. I walk in with $10,000. I leave with $9,000 and receipts showing that I bought a book for $2,000 and sold it for $9,000. When I walk in you have the book in inventory, and when I leave you still have the book and $1,000."

Sasha stood in silence for a while. He was confused and somewhat dumbfounded. Then it struck him. He would be in effect providing a money trail for Hugo's gambling winnings: money laundering. Then his brain kicked in and he considered the proposition. He started to think, but out loud.

"It doesn't hold up. Your receipts would show that I had sold you a $10,000 book for $2,000. Why would I do that? It wouldn't stand up to any scrutiny. And, besides, how do I account for the other $8,000 that suddenly appears?"

With a grin, Hugo said, "My example had lots of flaws, obviously. But, I am happy that you thought through the problems and challenges, rather than just throwing me out. Why don't you think about the concept and see if you can come up with some ideas for us working together. I'll come back next week."

"OK, I guess."

With that Hugo left and Sasha was left standing in a bit of shock. Nevertheless, he worked his brain for ideas. He didn't go to the pub that Friday.

The following Monday, Hugo returned.

After a few preliminaries, Sasha said, "I have some thoughts but they may not work. It depends somewhat on what you can arrange as well."

"Tell me."

"The problem I had was how we can work your idea with that extra money in the system. Accountants and tax inspectors could create issues. The answer may be in creating a phantom book. You buy it. You sell it to me. I sell it to a phantom customer. You again end up with a money trail up to the amount I supposedly pay you. I end up with a paper profit equal to the commission you are paying me. Of course we will both be paying taxes on our paper gains."

"Who do I buy this phantom book from?"

"At least to start we can pretend that it came from my old bookstore, Bye Buy Books. I happen to have some old invoice books in my files."

"Then, I declare the supposed profit on my taxes?" asked Hugo.

"Right, it's just as if you declared your original money on taxes, but now it's open and legal."

"How strange will it be that I am suddenly buying and selling a rare book?"

"I don't know what other businesses you have or how you manage your income and taxes but you should probably set yourself up as a book scout in some entity. Those are people who actually do scour out-of-the-way book shops, antique malls, estate sales, whatever, looking for cheap books that have value to a better book dealer. That's what we would be creating on paper."

"I can do that. I do have a few enterprises."

"There is one other thing, Hugo,"

"What's that?"

"I need more than a ten percent margin. After all, I am doing the laundry; all of the paper trail comes from me. I am most vulnerable to being found out."

Hugo stared at him. He hadn't expected push back, but then he hadn't been at all sure if Sasha was going to be a willing player and was going to create a viable scheme.

"Fifteen percent?"

"I was thinking twenty."

After a pause, Hugo said, "OK, twenty to start. But we may need to change that when we see how things develop and what problems we find."

"It's a deal."

For the next while, every two weeks they would get together and create the paperwork for ten to fifteen thousand dollars' worth of fabricated sales.

After a couple of months, they realized that the paper records they were creating were too simple and too repetitive to stand up to real scrutiny.

Sasha then worked with Hugo to create a few new book dealer names, register them, and organize online accounts where books could be sold. It was a new wrinkle. They could post their fake books and buy them through Hugo's account, creating a much more elaborate paper trail. To further legitimize the process, Sasha even moved some real books to those new entities and sold them to actual online customers.

After four months, they reached a milestone. They had processed $100,000 of value.

11

They were sitting in the Metro Rare Books store after closing hours one evening, having just finished their latest batch of paperwork for the recent transactions.

Hugo had been in a sour mood since he arrived. He had moaned, "Why do I take bets on golf? It should be easy. The fields are big and many different players win. The bettors always over-bet the favorites. Then they win anyway. Last month Annika Sorenstam won the LPGA Championship. Now Tiger Woods won the British Open again, his tenth major. Too many people bet on them both."

Sasha worked to change the topic. "Things have gone OK for us so far."

"You know," said Hugo, picking up on the topic. "'I know a couple of other people that could be interested in joining this process. We could expand."

"It would be great to do that. We create a lot of paper and set up a bunch of risk for the amount of money involved. It's been good to get an extra $20,000 over four months, but after taxes it doesn't really make a big change in things."

"Should I talk to them?"

"No, our activities don't really lend themselves to a larger scale. If a whole bunch more money appeared we could get detected. At the current level we sort of float under the radar. My book business isn't a great profit maker but it has a decent amount of cash flow in and out. It covers our current activities."

"What else can we do? Do you have any more ideas?"

"I've been trying to come up with something new. Of course the real solution would be if we could find some valuable books at a low price. Then we could sell them to the market and get outsiders' money into our system. We could flow your money through those transactions and I could clean up the real money through internal paperwork."

"Right."

"Did you see the story in the news recently where some fellow actually stole dozens, if not hundreds, of maps from the libraries at such places as Harvard and Yale and other big libraries? They were worth millions. Those places have lots of very valuable books for sure. Too bad we can't get some."

"Do you mean drive a truck up to the front doors and haul away a bunch of books?" Hugo laughed.

"Hardly. They're tucked away in special rooms and have some real security I assume. The map thief stole them one at a time over a long period, thus going undetected."

"So, how do we do that?"

"Can't happen. First of all, the security and book handling procedures are surely going to be tightened after these map thefts. Books are much harder to take. They're bulky. Besides, you have to sign them out and return them before you leave the special areas. The map guy just cut a map out of a book or atlas and then returned it. No one checked for a missing page."

"Too bad."

"Maybe I should get a job at one of those places and take books out in my lunch bucket?"

"Or…"

"Or, what?"

"Maybe we can find someone who already works there and have him do it for us."

"Sure, and maybe Santa Claus or the Easter Bunny will deliver them to us."

12

The next Monday Hugo walked into the bookstore with another person. He was shorter and older than Hugo, but he walked with an air of confidence. He wore a well-tailored suit and his shoes shone from a high gloss polish. Hugo appeared deferential, even as he opened the door to the shop.

Hugo introduced him, "This is Mr. Esposito. Tony."

Sasha immediately sensed a serious tone and resisted saying something like, "How is retirement from hockey?" This guy had probably never skated in his life and certainly didn't look like he had an easy sense of humor.

"How do you do, Mr. Esposito," he said, not sure he should even use Tony.

"Fine thanks. It's Tony."

Hugo interjected, "I have been telling Tony about our business and our conversation last week and he has some ideas for us."

Sasha just nodded, not quite sure what he was about to hear.

Tony spoke.

"First, I would like to hear more about the type of books that are in the fancy collections in the big libraries. How many are there? How valuable are they? Can they truly be marketed?"

Sasha responded to those questions and many more for at least an hour. There were tens of thousands of books in the major libraries. Many were worth tens of thousands of dollars; some were worth hundreds of thousands; a few were worth millions. By careful and patient selling, via a reputable dealer such as himself, and being willing to leave profits for others, most books could be sold. Beware of any books that have unique individual characteristics. Of course, they are in secure areas and watched while being used by outsiders for research. The libraries were being accessed less and less all the time due to digitization. Budgets and staff levels were being reduced. And on it went.

Then Tony said, "What if I could gain access to some of those books? What would we do?"

Sasha glanced up at Hugo with a questioning look.

Hugo nodded.

"Well, I assume Hugo has briefed you on our little operation to date. We would scale it up with added dimensions.

"First of all, we could enter the books into the system in a series of moves via various sites that we control, especially online ones, where your entities could participate in the chain of ownership, thereby creating legitimate paths for your funds to emerge at the end when the books are actually sold to real customers with outside money. Meanwhile, the actual funds would enter another sequence of false or inflated sales by the organizations. They would then emerge at an after-tax value."

"How many books could we process at a time?"

"That is probably the greatest risk. The sudden emergence of very valuable books in the market gets noticed; too many gets too much notice. To start with, I would say one book a month, maybe two if they are in totally different areas of interest to collectors, until we test everything out. The sales will need to be surrounded by legitimate books of similar value in the sites, and those are also hard to find, although we could probably buy and sell books from other dealers at a small or no margin to cover our activities."

"Thanks. I will decide if and how to proceed," said Tony.

Sasha swallowed hard before he asked his main question.

"How does that work, generally? What are our risks?"

Tony smiled. "Sir, I don't think you want to know the details, but be assured I always find that in my business honey works better than vinegar in a long-term relationship."

13

Two months later, after one of their regular meetings, Hugo said, "What would be your first choice of books from the Woodbridge Heritage Institute?"

"What!!!"

"We might have an opening."

Again, "What? Are you serious?"

"Yes. It's not open-ended though. We need to specify a book that is small, valuable, but not astronomically so, and is related to a subject where the likelihood of someone actually asking to see it is low."

Sasha looked at Hugo in disbelief.

"How did that happen?"

"I don't know and I doubt if you really want to know. What do the politicians call it? Credible denial?"

"If there is a source, couldn't they suggest something?"

"At this point, apparently, we want to establish some control and besides we need to know that the item is really marketable."

"The WHI has one of the largest rare book collections in the world. This could be like a kid in a candy shop."

"Be sure to take it seriously, and think it through. This is our first big test. Apparently the WHI holdings are public knowledge. They have a web site where everything is listed; after all, their stated mandate is to make knowledge available to everyone. Look at it."

"OK."

At that point Sasha realized that Hugo was a deeper individual than he projected. He recalled him saying that he had a few enterprises. Maybe all the Friday bar wagering was just a distraction.

Anyway, he went online to the WHI website.

"A kid in a candy store? No. More like a kid in Santa's Workshop," he thought.

He spent hours poring through the listings, trying to meet all the criteria. He wasn't sure what the requirement for being small was. Of course there were many large books, atlases, multi-volume sets that would not qualify, but what of a relatively normal book, octavo in size, maybe an inch or so thick? There were many of those. But, he remembered his frivolous conversation with Hugo a couple of months earlier when they joked about putting a book in a lunch bucket. He kept looking.

Then he found it.

It was perfect.

It was small, maybe six inches by four inches and less than an inch thick. It was quite rare and thus valuable to collectors. It was a first edition in original covering boards, not rebound. The text had been reprinted many times over the almost four hundred years of its existence, and thoroughly analyzed by historians. It was unlikely to be requested by researchers.

It had, perhaps, the longest title of any book; certainly so for a small book. *The Strange and Dangerous Voyage of Captain Thomas James in his Intended Discovery of the North-West Passage into the South Sea in the years 1631 and 1632 wherein the Miseries Endured both in Going, Wintering and Returning, and the Rarities Observed.* It was published in 1633.

It described the voyage by Thomas James into Hudson Bay in the 1630s looking for a possible opening to a Northwest Passage to the Pacific. It was the definitive voyage to prove that no such passage existed out of Hudson Bay. Explorers would need to look farther north.

Its market value was certainly over one hundred thousand dollars, perhaps twice that to the right buyer.

He called Hugo and gave him the information.

Three weeks later, Hugo walked into the bookstore with a package and an envelope. In the package was the James book. In the envelope was one hundred thousand dollars in cash.

"OK, Mr. Magic. Do your thing."

It took some time but all went smoothly.

He quickly moved the listing and supposed sale of the book through a series of bookselling sites, first one of his phantom online listings and then through a couple of sites that were controlled by Hugo and his associates. Finally the last site sold it into the marketplace through an online listing. They priced it at $125,000 and sold it to a reputable major dealer for a 20% discount at $100,000. Within a short while they saw that dealer advertise the book in his monthly catalogue for $140,000.

Meanwhile the $100,000 in cash was deployed to buy and resell legitimate books. From online sites and from other dealers' catalogues that were easily accessible, he bought five books ranging from $10,000 to $40,000. He then quickly moved them through his online site that had the James book briefly, to give it some camouflage. He even sold three of them publically from that site. He moved the other two back to his own shop and sold them over a few weeks, one to an unknown online customer and one to another dealer. The five books sold for $120,000, not a big profit but adequately recovering the discount he had got on the purchase and, more importantly providing a trail of sales and support for the James sale.

So at the end of the day, having started with the $100,000 of Hugo and Tony's cash and the stolen James book, they ended up with $200,000 of laundered money. Sasha got $40,000, half for laundering the cash and half for marketing the James.

A similar process happened every month or so for the next year.

14

Then one day Hugo walked into the store, again accompanied by Tony Esposito, He hadn't seen Tony in over a year, not since their first meeting.

After a few preliminaries, Tony said, "We are thinking about expanding our operations. Triple."

"Oh! Won't that greatly increase our risk of exposure?"

"We don't think so. It seems the book-dealer and book-collecting world accept these books without asking too many questions, once you have done your shuffling. They seem anxious to find these good books."

"But, my exposure will increase with all of the extra activity."

"I don't think that is a big worry. You are covering your tracks pretty well and paying taxes on the gains. Maybe you will have to just stash some away for retirement but so what."

"Don't the authorities try to watch you and your activities?"

"Yes, but not too aggressively. First of all, we provide a service to our customers and no one ever complains to the authorities. Second, trying to track down money washing is a very low priority for them. I don't even like to call it money washing or money laundering, it's really money liberating. All that hidden money comes into the open and pays taxes. You are actually doing a public service."

Sasha couldn't help laughing out loud at that. People can rationalize anything that serves them well, he thought.

"What about the source of the books? That could draw attention if we do too many."

"We have developed two new sources."

This gave him pause. He wasn't sure he wanted to know about that part of the business, but obviously the look on his face showed concern.

"Relax," said Tony. "It's all smooth. Let me tell you a little about it to calm your concerns. After our first meeting and based on the things you told me about the book business, we did some deeper looking. As you had said, the institutions had large collections but they were being used sporadically and their staff levels were not very high. We checked out salaries and found that they were pretty modest. Young people with advanced university degrees in history and library science couldn't find much work except at such places and their salaries were quite low.

"Then we just had to find someone who would like to make extra money and was willing to take a few books for us. Our business can tend to find potential candidates, who generally are people in over their heads in debt, either through gambling or taking out too many high-interest loans.

"Once we found a very likely person, we approached him with an offer of debt forgiveness and a reasonable fee for each book. It took a while for him to digest it all, but the temptation was too great. Actually he has become quite creative in taking books and covering his tracks. And of course he has no reason to go to the authorities; he is totally involved and compromised. There was no coercion used, just temptation.

"Now we have two more."

15

"Yes," Sasha thought. "That's how it all started years ago. It has been a great ride."

He had made a lot of money, much of it openly declared and tax paid, some of it tucked away for the future in things like gold coins. He even had some Bitcoin but didn't really understand that or trust it.

It had been easy to bring the extra cash into his system. Beyond just fabricating some fake buys and sells of books, it was easy to adjust records so that he appeared to buy real books for bigger discounts and sell them for higher premiums, thus inflating his apparent margins.

But, what to do now? They had developed five places where they obtained books over the years but there had been recent FBI inquiries at some of them. Their sources had passed that information on to Tony's contact and Hugo had told him. They were obviously concerned.

They had stopped all of their operations for a while and nothing else happened. It was as if it had all gone away. Could that be true?

Hugo came into the store the next week.

"What are you thinking?" he asked. "We've laid low for three months now and everything seems quiet. Even a couple of our sources, who were very nervous originally, are asking about restarting. I guess they've become used to the extra money."

"OK. Let's start again but tell everyone to be very careful."

"Fine. Anything else?"

"Yes. Tell the sources to concentrate on books related to Arctic exploration in the 1800s. There's a significant increase in collector interest in those right now. It has been stimulated by the recent discovery of John Franklin's ships that were lost in the mid-1800s, well over 150 years ago. The original search for those ships stimulated much of the Arctic exploration and publications in the later 1800s."

BOOK THREE

The Franklin Connection

16

Agent Wilson was in his Washington office. His phone rang and the person on the other end identified herself as Rhonda Wright, the Director of Rare Books at the Woodbridge Heritage Institute.

"Agent Wilson, you visited us here at the WHI about a year ago. At that time I said we were not aware of any significant thefts or missing books in our collection. That may have changed."

"Dr. Wright, you are obviously disturbed. Tell me more."

"As I recall telling you, we have hundreds of thousands of books and it is absolutely impossible to conduct a total inventory check. However, recently we were looking to gather together a group of books to create a special display and we discovered that a number of important books could not be found. I decided to call you before we did anything more."

"Good. If we assume that someone in your organization could be involved in the books going missing, it's best not to stir things up too much until we can formulate a plan of investigation."

"Well, the fact that we have missing books is pretty well known by our key staff members, as a number of them were involved in gathering them up."

"Of course; just don't do anything else too proactively for now."

"I can do that."

"Can you give me more information about the missing books?"

"Simply put, they relate to Arctic exploration in the 1800s. As some background, there have been some exciting discoveries in the past few years. The long-lost ships of Sir John Franklin, a famous Arctic explorer, were found by a consortia of the Canadian government and a group of geographic and history associations who had spent years looking. This is more than 150 years after they went missing.

"Many other explorers looked for Franklin and his ships for years after he went missing. They never found his ships but they created many fascinating journals and books and maps of the unfolding knowledge of the far north. These are of historical significance due to the new knowledge they contained. They are also valuable collectors' items for the same reason.

"The renewed awareness of Franklin and the discovery of his ships has stimulated a large uplift in demand for those items. It has also created a significant public interest in the Franklin story. For example, the National Museum at Greenwich, England, probably the epicenter of English exploration for centuries, organized a major display and information program related to the Franklin expedition after the ships were discovered.

'Now, there is a large event planned to celebrate the discovery of the ships in Canada. It's going to be held in Ottawa, the Canadian capital. It's expected that the government will be putting many artifacts that have been found on display and will provide more information about the search effort that found them. They might even reveal where the ships actually are. That has been kept secret to prevent curiosity seekers and looters from getting to them.

"There are going to be many activities and events: political speeches and festival activities; public displays and historical seminars; and an antiquarian book fair complemented by a public auction of rare books.

"We at the WHI had decided that we would support this event. We have a large collection of Arctic books and artifacts that could make an impressive display. Our motives were manifold, not the least of which was to give our existence a higher profile, maybe to a newer generation. The use of our institute's resources has been falling off over the years, as we discussed in your earlier visit. That's why we started to round up Arctic books and how we discovered the holes in our collection."

"That's useful," said Wilson. "I will need to organize a few things here but I would like to come and meet with you and determine how we best proceed. I can be there next Monday; can you sit tight that long?"

"Yes, I have informed the President of the Institute of the situation and he agreed that we would wait for your instructions."

After hanging up the phone, Wilson thought, "Well, first I need to tell Director Stephens. I know she will just smile at me with a knowing look and then say, 'Go get it.'

"Then I need to round up the team, get some people started on background research into all the things I heard from Dr. Wright, and get organized to return to the WHI with Wilma Watkins.

"Maybe this will be our breakthrough."

17

Agents Wilson and Watkins met with Dr. Wright, the Director of Rare Books at the WHI the next Monday. She was probably in her late-40s, tall, slim and dressed in a well-tailored business suit.

After the expected pleasantries, Rhonda Wright repeated the general overview of the situation that she had given Wilson on the phone.

Then they dug deeper into the details. Wilma Watkins led the questioning, as she was the expert in art and antiquities and she had spent most of the past few days researching more information about rare books, Arctic exploration and John Franklin.

"Exactly how many books are missing?" she asked.

"All we know at this time is that when we set out to round up about 100 books for our planned display at the Franklin event in Ottawa we could not locate ten of them. We haven't looked any deeper into our total Arctic collection or other areas yet. Once I called Agent Wilson, I decided to hold off on any further actions until we met today."

"What is the value of those books?"

"We don't actually keep track of the current market value of our collections. We have a huge number of books and have had some of them for decades. Updating current valuations would be impossible. However, we are aware of general trends in the markets, as we are buying and appraising donations constantly. I would guess the ten missing books are worth as much as a half-million dollars, maybe more. We can get a current estimate done by an expert when we decide to expand our actions."

"Are you sure they are really missing?"

"It's always possible some of them have been misfiled or are out on loan, but we did a preliminary check on the obvious places and found nothing. I think they are gone."

"Do you have any suspicions about who might have taken the books?"

"That's the toughest question. I have done a lot of thinking about that over the past few days and I have no idea who could do something like this."

"How many people work at the WHI?"

"The WHI is a large operation with over one hundred employees. However, the Rare Books Division has about ten employees. There's myself, the Assistant Director, two curators, two administrators, a researcher, a restorer and usually a couple of interns."

"You mentioned that you have hundreds of thousand books. That doesn't seem like a large staff."

"Well, the fact is that most of our books sit on our shelves undisturbed for years. Actually, I am currently being asked to find ways to reduce the staff numbers. Budgets are under pressure."

"How is the security of the area managed?"

"There is a check-in desk at the entrance to the rare books section, usually staffed by one of the interns. They check bags, briefcases and the like of anyone entering or leaving the area. People who want to take a book to a reading kiosk need to sign it out on a card left at the desk and then return the book to the desk when leaving."

"Can anyone come and go?"

"Well, in theory I guess, but it's not like we're a public library that lets anyone take away books. Not that many people actually come to the area, and those that do are almost always researchers or graduate students working on their study programs. Sometimes staffers from other areas of the WHI come in to get information that might be related to their specialties."

"Do books actually leave the area?"

"Sometimes. Senior staff working on projects sometimes take books out to work with in evenings or days off. We have a special procedure for that. A form is completed in triplicate. One copy goes in a file where it is kept until the book is returned. One copy is taken and put in another file at security when the book leaves. The third copy is left with the book and is matched to the ones in the files when the book is returned. Also, at times an outside senior researcher or someone like that can make a special request, perhaps to compare something in our collection to something somewhere else. In those cases, I would usually need to sign off and it would be very carefully recorded."

"How hard would it be for a staff member to just take a book away?"

"When I tried to visualize that I decided that if someone was really careful they could probably take a book out of the rare books area. They would also need to take it out of the building of course. We do have basic security screening at the entrances to the building but a book wouldn't set off a metal detector and I must admit the screening of bags and briefcases for well-known staffers is probably quite cursory. Perhaps you should also talk to our Head of Security."

"How can you proceed to determine how widespread the problem of missing books is?"

"As I said earlier, it's a daunting task. I think the next step would be to take inventory of all of our Arctic and Antarctic exploration books. That's the area where we have detected a known problem; ten books missing out of a hundred books that we were trying to gather up."

"Then what?"

"Our collection is organized into many major categories such as Science, Medicine, Philosophy, Nature, etc. The next step would be to pick a topic and check it out and so on."

"Who would do that work? Your staff? That might be like asking the foxes to count the chickens."

"When I talked with the President of the WHI we anticipated the need to do this. He agreed that this is a big enough concern that we could hire a group of interns, probably students from the local university, to do the checking in teams of two; after all, it is primarily a record checking exercise."

"OK," said Wilson, summing up what had been discussed. "You should start on the further inventory taking. We will want to interview your security manager and the members of your staff. They all know that books are missing and so we won't be revealing anything new to them by talking to them. Then we will determine what to do next."

"OK, I'll call in Brian Webb, our Head of Security."

18

As Agents Wilson and Watkins waited for the security man to arrive they briefly chatted. Rhonda Wright had left the meeting room they had been using.

"What do you think?" asked Wilson.

"I don't know. Ten books out a sample of a hundred seems significant. It's certainly worth digging deeper."

"I agree."

With that, Brian Webb arrived. They greeted each other and all sat down around the meeting room table.

"Mr. Webb," began Wilson, "we are obviously here in response to the missing rare books. What can you tell us?"

Brian Webb was in his mid-50s, medium height and slightly overweight. He wore a checkered sport coat over a pale yellow shirt with a patterned tie. To Wilson and Watkins he stood out as a retired policeman, which he was. He appeared a little nervous and seemed somewhat defensive in his initial responses.

"I'm surprised that there may be missing books. It's a relatively quiet operation here and people are checked in and out."

"How is the security set up?"

"We always have staff at the entrances. People walk through a scanner system and all bags and parcels are inspected. To tell you the truth, with all the events in public places these days such as bombings, shootings, what-have-you, I admit we are probably more focused on what people bring in than what they take out."

"Have you had any incidents?"

"No, not really. Maybe the odd minor thing, but nothing serious."

"What about staff members and after-hours?"

"They are checked as well. After hours, everyone exits by a side door off the main entrance. It leads to the parking lot."

"Do you have any cameras set up for surveillance?"

"Yes, at the main entrances and at various places around the building."

"Are they monitored?"

"No, we don't have that kind of staff. They record on a multi-day cycle and are available to look at if we have an incident."

"Do you look at them often?"

"Hardly ever. Maybe a couple of times a year, usually when there is some minor disagreement between a visitor and a staff member over the use of something or disturbing a display. Again, minor things."

"How hard would it be for a staff member to take out a book?"

Webb squirmed a bit. "Everyone is checked, but I have to admit it is probably somewhat cursory with staff members who are well known to our security screeners. This isn't that big of a place, staff-wise."

"Is there anyone on staff that you might consider as a likely, or even possible suspect?"

'No, no one stands out to me, and I have been thinking about that."

"Thank you for talking with us Mr. Webb. I am sure we will have more questions when we get deeper into our investigation."

"Sure, fine."

After he left, Wilma Watkins looked at Wilson, shook her head, and said, "If someone inside has been taking books, they certainly wouldn't have any difficulty in getting them out of this building."

19

Over the next two days the FBI agents interviewed the staff members of the rare books section. This included the Assistant Director, Katherine Clay; the two curators, Jillian Granger and Dennis Davis; the researcher, Timothy Foulks; the restorer, Emma Johnston; and the administrative staff. The interviews were remarkably similar.

Dennis Davis, one of the curators, was the third interview. He was in his mid-40s, and looked the librarian stereotype with a small moustache and goatee.

Wilma Watkins again took the lead.

"Thank you for seeing us, Mr. Davis. Obviously we want to talk about the missing books."

"That's fine. Call me Dennis. What can I tell you?"

"What do you think has happened here?"

"I don't know. We are all amazed that books could be missing. We have checked the records and have looked for places where they could have been alternatively filed but have found nothing."

"Tell us how the rare books area is organized and the roles everyone has."

"Dr. Wright is our Director. She oversees the whole group and signs off on major items. However, she also spends a lot of her time on external activities, notably cultivating wealthy collectors and donors who might be benefactors of the WHI. Nowadays we get more books from donors than we can purchase with our budget.

"Katherine Clay is the Assistant Director and she really runs the everyday operations, providing supervision and guidance to the rest of us.

"Jillian Granger and I are the senior curators. We evaluate new books for completeness and value; we organize the collections; we document the books, and so on.

"Timothy Forbes is the staff researcher. He is usually working in collaboration with outside professors doing joint research from our extensive collections.

"Emma Johnston is our restorer. Books, especially when they first arrive, often need repairs and clean-up. Emma does that. She also coordinates with outside, commercial restorers when major work is required.

"The administrators and interns keep the files, organize the books, and do the routine activities, including the interface with outsiders who come to access our books."

"How do you and Jillian divide up the work?"

"It's not actually formalized but we generally focus on different areas. I tend to focus on the areas like Science, Medicine and Nature. She tends to focus more on topics like History, Philosophy and Politics. However, there are many overlaps and we work closely together."

"Have you ever taken books out of WHI?"

"Yes, a few times. Sometimes I am working on a research or compilation project that has a deadline and so I'll take a book or two home for a few days. Sometimes I'm working on a personal article for a magazine or specialist publication and will similarly take out some books. There is always a desire to publish papers in our business. In any case, the procedure for taking books out by staff members is quite precise; it involves a form in triplicate that is vetted by security."

"How difficult would it be to take books out surreptitiously?"

"Some of us have actually talked about that lately, not with Rhonda or Katherine of course, but among ourselves. If you were very careful it could probably be done; security isn't that diligent."

"Is that what you think has happened?"

"Who knows? But, what would someone do with the books afterwards? Sure, they can be valuable but how could you actually sell them? I could hardly go to a book dealer or auction house with a rare book and expect them to pay me high amounts without asking lots of questions. It doesn't make sense to me, but I guess the fellow at the Carnegie did something like that."

After they had finished their first round of interviews Wilson and Watkins huddled again.

Wilma said, "Everyone was quite consistent with their stories and perspectives. I don't mean in an apparent rehearsed way; just they all seemed open and sincere. I didn't detect anything suspicious."

"Agreed, but people can be good at telling a story if they have had time to rehearse it."

"Who knows what financial pressures or jealousies or frustrations might motivate someone. We have heard that salaries in this area aren't that high and there are possible pending staff cuts. The Director seems competent and is still quite young; others may not see a path forward to future promotion. Just being surrounded by valuable things could be an irresistible temptation."

"I think our next step is to get the local office to deploy a couple of field agents to do some background checks and financial profiles of the staff. Who knows what they might find."

"And, in a while we will get the results of the extended audits of some of the other book areas and learn if the problem is widespread."

20

Two weeks later Wilson and Watkins returned to WHI.

However, on the way, they first stopped at the local FBI office to find out what the field agents had learned about the staff members. They met in a small conference room with Agents Karl Kolby and Ernie Haas.

Kolby started. "We did a routine first-level background and financial check on the eight people you interviewed. You know, where they lived, what cars they drove, what other large assets they had like RVs or boats, etc. We also tested whether they were known to have any extravagant habits or travels. Were they gamblers?"

Hass elaborated. "Of course, we were trying to keep a low profile and so the questions were very general when we talked to people like neighbours, bank managers, etc."

Watkins interrupted. "How do you ask a bank manager a low profile question about high lifestyles or gambling by one of their customers?"

Hass smiled. He realized that Watkins hadn't done much street work; she was a specialist.

"We keep it general, but with a focus. We always have a cover story such as the person is being considered for an award or is being profiled in a newspaper article or alumni publication. We don't always need to identify ourselves as being FBI. In those circumstances, people volunteer a lot of information, sometimes even bragging on the person rather than covering anything up."

"So, what did you find?"

"You have a bunch of low profile, steady people with few anomalies. In other words, a bunch of stereotypical librarians."

"Can you elaborate?"

"No one seemed to be living beyond their income. The only one with a fancy car is the Director, who has a Porsche Boxster, not inconsistent with her income. The curator, Jillian Granger, took a large European vacation last year, but she had inherited some money from her mother and the trip seemed to be consistent with that."

"Did any other type of motive surface?"

"The Assistant Director, Katherine Clay, who is older than Rhonda Wright and was passed over for the Director position a few years ago, apparently was upset at the time but people think that has passed and she has settled down into being a good overseer.

"The curator, Dennis Davis, who is about the same age as the Director has expressed some frustration but that's about all. He seems to be well respected. He might have had a gambling issue in the past but it appears to be long gone."

"Anything else?"

"The restorer and the administrators had nothing of interest show up. The researcher, Timothy Forbes, does appear to hobnob, maybe freeload a bit, with outside academics and researchers but we couldn't find anything more. It appears he might be anxious to have something significant published, even in collaboration with others."

"Your conclusion?"

"With the level of work we did, there was nothing suspicious or even attention-grabbing."

21

Their next stop was to see the Director at the WHI.

They were shown into the conference room where Rhonda Wright was waiting for them along with Katherine Clay, her Assistant Director.

Wilson frowned a bit, betraying his FBI training, which Wright picked up on.

"Katherine has joined us because she has been providing the supervision and guidance to the ongoing audits. We didn't want to involve anyone else on staff."

Wilson nodded.

Katherine Clay spoke up then.

"Over the past two weeks we have been able to audit six other categories of our collection. We recruited six students from the university with the help of the Dean of Humanities. We figured that we should get the best students we could, and knew they would appreciate the extra cash. History and English students don't get the same summer jobs as engineers and financial specialists. They worked diligently and carefully in teams of two.

"They covered a range of different topics that was manageable in a week's effort, meaning cross-checking records and inventories of about one thousand books per group, some smaller, some larger.

"As well as finishing the Arctic Exploration group, they analyzed 18th Century Philosophy, 19th Century Medicine, Australian History, South American Botany, WWI Politics and Modern Physics. We decided that was a wide sample to test."

"And?" said Agent Watkins, a little impatiently.

"We discovered two more Arctic books missing. In the other categories there were one or two missing books."

"What do you take that to mean?"

Director Wright spoke up.

"I was amazed at how few books were not found. Our collections go back many decades. Each group has hundreds, if not thousands, of books. It's inevitable that some get misplaced. If we had been gathering anything but the Arctic exploration group for a display, a couple of missing books in one area would not have attracted a lot of attention and I would not even have called you. It was the ten out of one hundred that is the anomaly. I don't know what that means."

Wilson then spoke up, detecting a change of tone from Director Wright.

"How will you proceed next?"

"We will give you the best descriptions possible of the missing Arctic books. Hopefully, you will be able to trace some. Then you will have leads that might let you backtrack to their sourcing trail."

"Are you going to take inventory of your other collections?"

"No, we don't see the point. The sample we did showed minor discrepancies. We don't have the resources or inclination to do more of that."

"But, even a few books per category could mean hundreds of books."

"Statistically insignificant. Our President and his Management Committee have reviewed all of this and see no point in chasing it any further. A few missing books due to administrative slipups or bad filing shouldn't taint the integrity of the whole collection."

"Or does that mean taint the reputation of the WHI with donors and supporters?" Wilson said, pointedly.

Rhonda Wright looked Wilson directly in his eyes and simply said, "Thank you for all of your assistance and advice. Katherine will provide you with the descriptions of the Arctic books. I hope you can find them."

She turned and left the room.

Wilma Watkins, trying to save something out of the situation, said, "Katherine, could we also get the descriptions of the missing books in the other categories? You never know what might turn up as a connection."

After a pause, "Sure, why not?"

22

Wilson returned to Washington and set up a briefing meeting with the FBI Director, Sybil Stephens. He reviewed the events of the past couple of weeks and summarized the situation.

"After pursuing what seemed like a plausible breakthrough from the WHI, we have come to a bit of a dead end. The WHI isn't cooperating much anymore and we didn't uncover any obvious leads."

"What can you do next?" asked the Director.

"All we have thought of are a couple of long shots. We need to decide whether they're worth dedicating the time and resources."

"What are they?"

"The first and easiest thing to do is to send out some kind of general notice or announcement to the major libraries and institutions telling them that there are some indications that books related to Arctic exploration are being stolen and warn them to be diligent. We wouldn't identify the WHI, which I am sure would not give us permission. However, that was the only area where we have some indicators of a problem and it may turn up other leads. We know the institutions are not inclined to do any total audits but this might stimulate them to do a limited check. If we do get some responses, we'll need to follow up with staff work and analysis, which could just be more dead ends."

"Still, that is relatively easy, and might surface something. Do it. What else?"

"We do have the list and description of the dozen Arctic books missing from the WHI. If we could find one or two we could perhaps back-trace the path it has followed. We know there is going to be the major celebration of Arctic exploration in Ottawa this summer, complete with a book fair and an auction. Attendance will be high. The books are valuable; maybe one will be there."

"That does seem like a longshot."

"Actually, even more so since the books are not singular; other copies of the same books exist and they are difficult to distinguish. The descriptions are pretty general, but an expert might be able to tell."

"Who could do that and how do you carefully inspect books at a book fair and auction?"

"We could recruit Herb Trawets, the retired dealer that President Cartwright recommended and who I first interviewed. He is knowledgeable and certainly appears above suspicion. Also, when we were investigating the fraudulent book that the President bought, I did attend a rare book fair and a large auction. The books are readily accessible for handling and inspection by anyone that's there, whether in dealers' display booths or at the pre-auction layout. We are just looking for a dozen different books, and they are rare. Even if there are a hundred dealers there, I doubt if there will be more than a couple of copies of each publication.

"Yes, it is a longshot and will cost time and money, including travel, but it's all we have right now."

As Wilson expected, since in effect the Director had started all of this, she said, "OK, plan for it. Perhaps, in the meanwhile, your notices to the other institutions may surface something new."

23

A few weeks earlier, Dennis Davis had been in a frenzy. Rhonda Wright, the Director of the WHI, had decided to create a major display of rare Arctic books and it was discovered that some were missing.

Of course Dennis knew that; he had stolen them.

Then the FBI arrived and started questioning everyone. At least with a few days of advanced awareness he had prepared himself quite well.

First, he had called his contact, just known as Alberto, and told him what was happening. Alberto, after obviously consulting with others, told him to prepare for questioning. Be prepared. Be calm. Be open. Relax... Sure!

Dennis had thoroughly reviewed what he had done and felt he had left no obvious traces He just had to avoid attracting attention to himself.

It had all started more than twelve years earlier. He was in his early 30s then, working diligently as a relatively new curator at the WHI, having started there after graduating with a Bachelor degree in English History and a Masters in Library Science. The WHI job was a plum catch for someone in his field and he had moved up into a good position. But, he didn't make very much money.

He had gotten into the habit of making sports bets each week with a local bookie, Joe, as much out of boredom on weekends as the excitement of betting. Somehow, over time, he got behind for a few thousand dollars with the bookie, who seemed OK carrying him, albeit charging high interest. His debt just steadily grew.

Then one day after work, a stranger approached him in his local pub. He said his name was Alberto. He was polite, but focused. "Mr. Davis, it seems as though you have run up quite a debt with my friend Joe. I would like to help you out."

Dennis's first reaction was one of concern, even fear. What had he gotten himself into? What was going to happen?

"What do you mean?" he said.

"Let's go talk somewhere quieter."

They had walked down to a local park and sat on a bench. It was early evening.

Alberto knew who he was, where he worked, what he did, how much he earned and, of course, his gambling debt.

"Mr. Davis, what I am going to propose is very simple. We will write off your debt and even pay you something extra if you just bring us a book from the WHI collection."

Dennis was flabbergasted. "Steal a book! From the WHI? Never. Impossible. Not me."

"Calm down and think about it. How are you going to pay your debt? What if the people at the WHI learn that you are a gambler who is deeply in debt to people like Joe? What of your reputation, your career?"

Dennis just sat frozen for a couple of minutes. Then, "I don't know how I could even do it if I wanted to."

He watched as Alberto slightly smiled. He realized he had crossed a line when he went from "No" to "How."

"Go and think about it. Carefully. Meet me here again tomorrow evening."

All that night and the next morning Dennis was beside himself in disbelief and concern. What if he said no? If yes, how could he possibly do such a thing? Over and over.

The next evening he again met with Alberto.

"I am just not sure how I can do something like this. What book are we talking about?"

"I don't know that yet; I will need to find out."

"Well, you are certainly going to want something of value, but don't ask for something so rare that it gets easily noticed. Also, the smaller the better, no larger than octavo in size. Rare but obscure is also better so it doesn't get accessed often or at all."

"I'll get back to you."

A week later, Alberto walked into the pub again and handed Dennis a piece of paper. On it was written a single item: "James. Arctic Voyage. 1633."

Another week later, on a Friday evening after the WHI had been closed for a while and everyone in the rare books area had gone home, Dennis packed a lawyer's brief case, large and square, with a few books related to Elizabethan history. Hidden in a small compartment he had created at the bottom was the small James volume.

Approaching the security desk at the exit, he handed the triplicate forms to the security guard. He knew he was sweating and hoped his voice wouldn't crackle.

"Weekend reading, Dennis?"

Holding a handkerchief near his nose, he said, "I have a cold and so am staying in this weekend. Going to work on a paper for a Shakespeare-related publication."

The guard laughed, "A fun weekend for you, I guess. Not me; I'm going to a ball game tomorrow. Take care."

And with that, Dennis was out of the WHI.

The next day he gave the book to Alberto who said, "Great. You are clear with Joe." He also handed him an envelope with one thousand dollars in it.

Two weeks later, Alberto appeared in the pub again. "Let's talk."

Back to the park bench they went.

"We need another book."

"What? No! We are even and done. I am not betting anymore."

"Oh, Dennis. We can have such a great relationship and keep everything secret. You will get nicely rewarded."

The secrecy comment had its effect, both as an enticement and as a threat.

"What book this time?"

"Oh, we are going to let you decide. Valuable, of course."

And that was how it all started. Over the years, about once a month, Dennis would remove a book from the WHI. He varied the topics widely so not many books came from any given area.

He received about $3,000 per book, enough to help him but not enough to become too extravagant. In any case, he was careful. No flashy cars or jewelry. Any upscale vacations, such as Caribbean cruises, were never revealed to others at the WHI; he just went down to visit an imaginary sister in Florida.

He did remove some record cards from the files so some books would be harder to detect as missing. He did file a few books in wrong places, just as cover in case something happened. In fact, nothing happened.

Then, a year or so ago, there was a bit of a flurry as the FBI came to the WHI and asked about missing books in the aftermath of the Carnegie scandal that had become public. However, after they met with the Director nothing much else happened.

He had told Alberto about the FBI visit and questions, and they had stopped everything for a few months, but eventually resumed activity.

Then, in hindsight, they made a mistake. Acting on Alberto's instructions, over the past year he had focused on Arctic exploration books. The Director's decision to create an Arctic display exposed the large hole in the collection.

But, he did get prepared and apparently passed scrutiny with the FBI agents who interviewed him. He managed to be relaxed and open. He thought his acknowledgement that he did take books home at times, that he had discussed with others how books could be removed under their lax security, and his wonderment about how stolen books could be disposed of, all came off as credible.

Then they had the influx of students who audited a few other areas where a few books were missing. That led up to another visit from the FBI who talked with the Director and the Assistant Director.

Then, nothing. No more audits. No more questioning. It just all seemed to go away.

Dennis stopped taking books.

24

As soon as the WHI roundup of Arctic books started and the realization that books were missing set in, Dennis called Alberto, who called Tony, who called Hugo, who called Sasha.

They agreed that Tony and his network would alert the other four suppliers immediately and they would stop all future activity until they saw what actually unfolded.

There was a great deal of anxiety as they learned of the FBI involvement and the interview of Dennis. But then, after the second round of audits at the WHI everything became quiet again. Dennis reported that things seemed to be returning to normal at the WHI.

Although everyone was concerned, they also knew that there was limited knowledge of who was involved along the chain. Dennis only knew Alberto, who could quickly disappear if something happened to expose Dennis. Alberto knew Tony but didn't really know the extent of Hugo's involvement and didn't know anything about Sasha.

They then started to analyze the trail of books they had left. At the moment only the WHI missing Arctic books and a handful of others covering various topics were known to the authorities. They had all been moved through their various channels and finally sold online to other dealers or to direct customers. Some of those that were sold to other dealers had likely been sold further down the line.

None of the books were particularly unique and they had been cleaned up and sometimes modified slightly to reduce the chance anyone could identify them as coming from the WHI.

The only real risk, slight as it was, would be if someone did identify a book as coming from the WHI and they were able to backtrack it to one of their entities. As an extra precaution, they shut down a couple of the first-level online sites and had the inventory moved to new ones.

After a few more weeks passed, Alberto's suppliers at the other four institutions reported that a General Alert had been received via the American Rare Book Society. It said that there had been some reports of books related to Arctic Exploration being stolen. One of their suppliers, at the Baltimore Memorial Library, had taken three Arctic books over the previous months. The other three had not taken any. Fortuitously, in an ironic way, since Sasha initially had been disappointed that only the WHI actually had a large collection of Arctic exploration books.

When the Baltimore library did an inventory check they did discover that they were missing three Arctic books. It was a minor variance. They passed the information back to the ARBS. Nothing had happened as a follow up so far.

Sasha started to think about the upcoming Ottawa Arctic festival, complete with a book fair and an auction. It was the event that triggered the WHI discovery of its missing books. Should he go?

His first reaction was to stay far away from there. Why get noticed at all, if for some reason it was being monitored by the authorities due to the WHI connection?

But he was curious, and he really shouldn't attract any attention. It was going to be an open book fair, meaning that any accredited rare book dealer could participate. He was not a big player in the scheme of things; he belonged to his regional association and he often had booths at the various regional fairs. He did not have a high profile. He was not a member of the ABAA, the Antiquarian Booksellers Association of America, which tended to have the large players and which organized exclusive book fairs in places such as New York and California. He had met a few of the big players, since they sometimes came to regional fairs as well.

He had sold a few books to larger dealers at those fairs. That was the natural order of things. It was a bit ironic that he had probably sold more books to the larger dealers via his chain of stolen books with Hugo and Tony than directly to collectors.

He didn't specialize in Arctic books at all; he seldom had many in his normal inventory. Although the Ottawa event was focused on an Arctic theme, it wouldn't be unusual for a more general dealer to attend.

It would be easy to go online to check out known booksellers' catalogues and to search for Arctic books on general sites such as Abe Books or Bookfinder to fill out his selection.

His curiosity overcame his caution; he decided he would go to Ottawa.

In his online search for books to take to the Ottawa fair he discovered a copy of the 1633 Thomas James book related to Arctic exploration. It was a very new listing by a New England dealer that Sasha had never dealt with. Its price was $160,000. For some reason, he got nervous.

He knew that the James book very seldom appeared for sale. They had eventually sold the James from the WHI to a New York dealer for $100,000 and had seen him list it for $140,000. But that was over ten years ago. Could it be the same book resurfacing? It was the one book they had stolen that might be identifiable due to its true rarity. Could it end up in Ottawa? Could some authority on the lookout spot this new listing?

Without pausing to think through how plausible that might be, he picked up the phone and called the New England dealer. After a brief conversation he bought the book for $144,000. The dealer had balked at anything greater than a ten percent discount, citing its rarity and the newness of the listing. The tone in his voice betrayed a disappointment in giving any discount but he couldn't ethically refuse by the code of the dealers associations.

Sasha was satisfied. He was sure he could readily recover his cost with some time. If it was the same book that they had stolen from the WHI ten years ago, he had it back under control. For sure, that book was not going anywhere near Ottawa.

25

The *Franklin Festival of Arctic Celebrations* was the official title of the Ottawa event. It was organized by a composite group of government, academic and commercial organizations with the stated purpose of highlighting the significance of the Arctic to Canada, increasing knowledge of its history and celebrating the discovery of Sir John Franklin's lost ships.

The Canadian government was the primary sponsor and thus its location was Ottawa, Canada's capital. Some of the participants would have preferred a larger, more accessible city such as Toronto, but politics prevailed.

It was timed to coincide with Canada Day, July 1ˢᵗ, the annual recognition of Canada's independence as a nation. The normal celebratory activities, complete with political speeches and fireworks would kick off the festival. The Prime Minister would be front and center, always a good thing for a politician.

July 1ˢᵗ was midweek, which made it convenient for the multi-day festival to run into the weekend. Public displays related to the Arctic would be in the large Ottawa Convention Centre all week.

The Canada Day celebrations were on Wednesday. The Festival Gala Reception would be on Thursday, complete with a presentation on Franklin's history and his fate. The book fair would take place Friday and Saturday. The book auction would happen Friday afternoon.

People involved with the various displays would arrive first, early in the week, to set everything up.

The bookdealers would arrive by Thursday to set up their booths, although some did get there earlier to experience the other activities.

Also on Thursday the auction house would set up the books in a separate anteroom in the convention center for inspection by prospective buyers; it was their job to stimulate maximum interest.

26

Wilson had followed up on the ideas he had shared with the Director a few months earlier.

They had sent out an alert to many large libraries and institutions about the possible theft of books related to Arctic exploration but little had come of that. A couple of places reported a couple of missing books but no one considered it serious.

He had contacted Herb Trawets in California and explained what had happened and their thinking about the Ottawa book fair and auction.

Herb's reaction was one of total skepticism.

"Agent Wilson, these books are rare but not unique. They won't have any truly distinctive marks on them. Inevitably, anything that might slightly relate to WHI will have been cleansed or purged. They might even be trimmed or rebound. You seem to be dealing with knowledgeable people."

"I know. Still, there might be a chance. We don't know for sure how thorough the thieves are. Maybe they don't have those resources. The idea is that if we can find even one book we would have a lead for backtracking it. Right now we have nothing."

"What do you want me to do?"

"First, I'll send you a list and description of the books that are missing. That will be a dozen Arctic books from the WHI, as well as about ten other books on different topics. Also, there were a few other Arctic books reported missing from the alert we sent out. Look those over and then give me your synopsis of what we are looking for."

"OK, I can do that."

"Then, if we think there is any chance of finding one, we would like you to go to the Ottawa event and look at the books at the fair and in the auction."

"Maybe. Send me the list and we can talk again."

A week later, Herb called Wilson.

"Agent Wilson, I have looked at the lists and descriptions and done some research. It will definitely be a longshot."

"Tell me what you found."

"Certainly the books are antiquarian, rare and valuable, but those are relative terms. Most of the books would have a market value of $10,000 to $40,000 with a few higher. Most of them have copies available at a couple of sites online or have been publically sold by catalogue or auction over the past year. So, it will be tough to distinguish a specific copy.

"As well, the descriptions provided by the WHI are not very detailed. After all, they are cataloguing a collection, not trying to put together a sales brochure as a dealer would. General comments about some browning, or small tears, or slightly worn bindings will apply to almost every copy."

"Any glimmers of hope?"

"Glimmer? Maybe a slight halo in a fog bank. A couple of the books are more rare and valuable than the others. An example would be the published journal of Thomas James who explored Hudson's Bay in the 1600s. Any copy of it that we find would be worth a very close examination."

"Anything else?"

"Just an observation that all of the books are octavo size or smaller which would be consistent with someone sneaking them out of a secure location."

"What does octavo mean?"

"When books are printed it's done on relatively large pieces of paper. In the older centuries that wasn't exactly standardized but let's say it was approximately 20 inches by 24 inches. Then the large pages are folded into a smaller size, creating a small bundle that is bound together with other bundles to make a book. If the page is folded in half it has four surfaces of about twenty inches by twelve inches. That's called a folio size and is often used for atlases or illustration books. If the page is folded into four, that's a quarto about ten inches by twelve inches It was used for important books such as the journals of James Cook or George Vancouver. Fold it again into eight sheets with sixteen surfaces and you have an octavo, about ten by six. This became more and more the standard size by the mid-1800s. Those dimensions are approximate as the books were also trimmed to make them neat when bound. In any case, an octavo-sized book would be easier to conceal in a bag or a coat than something larger. None of the WHI missing books were larger than octavo."

"Interesting. Thanks, Mr. Trawets. Now, I know it might be a wild goose chase, but I would like you to join me in Ottawa and check out the books."

"I'll meet you there."

27

In preparation for the trip to Ottawa Agent Wilson needed to liaise with the Canadian RCMP to ensure that all international protocols were followed.

He had done something similar when he attended an antiquarian book auction in Vancouver while investigating the fake document linked to President Cartwright. By chance, the RCMP Inspector, Ian Fleming, was now stationed at the RCMP National Headquarters in Ottawa.

After clearing the contact with the appropriate channels in both countries, he placed a prescheduled call to Fleming.

"Chief Inspector Fleming, it's great to talk to you again. Congratulations on your promotion to Ottawa HQ."

"Hello, Agent Wilson. Thanks. As always in our business, perhaps a promotion and a relocation to HQ, especially from Vancouver to Ottawa, is a trade-off."

Wilson laughed, pleased that Fleming would be relaxed enough with him to say such a thing.

"For sure. What I'm calling about is that I am planning to come to Canada to attend the upcoming Franklin Arctic celebration in Ottawa and to scout out the antiquarian book fair and auction."

"That sounds like a repeat of your trip to Vancouver a couple of years ago."

"Yes and no. It's actually much simpler this time. We're trying to track down some valuable stolen books and there's a chance some of them might show up there. Unlike last time, I don't have any real leads on suspects and we won't likely be taking people aside for secret meetings."

"What can I do to help?"

"Right now, not much. I just wanted to give you a heads-up. I will be bringing a rare book expert with me and any activity will be dependent on what he finds."

"Fine. Let me know your schedule. Perhaps we can have dinner again; it was a very pleasant evening last time."

28

Agents Wilson and Watkins flew to Ottawa on the Wednesday, as did Herb Trawets. They met in their hotel lobby late that afternoon. Chief Inspector Fleming joined them.

After introductions were made, they made their way to the hotel's lounge and found a quiet table in a corner. They weren't particularly concerned about being seen; there was no way anyone could connect them to anything in particular. A waiter took their drink orders.

"The city is certainly busy," observed Herb.

"Sure is," replied Fleming. "With all of the Canada Day celebrations this is always a busy time. It's the official start of summer and the tourists flock to the capital. Tonight's fireworks will be spectacular as always."

"The Franklin exhibitions and the rare books events must add to the scope of things," commented Watkins.

"The exhibitions, definitely. People are intrigued by the Franklin story and the discovery of the shipwrecks. The book events are a nice addition, and I know that's why you're here. In reality, they are small attractions compared to the whole panoply of activities. A hundred bookdealers and a cluster of avid rare book collectors are dwarfed by the thousands of tourists, let alone the local citizens who love the Canada Day festivities. The Ottawa area has over one million people."

"Thanks again for joining us," said Wilson. "As I mentioned on the phone, we are on a bit of a blind scavenger hunt. Some rare books related to the Arctic are missing and we are hoping some might surface here. Herb is a retired antiquarian book dealer and he will be our main scout. Herb, tell us what you have in mind."

"Certainly. I have studied the descriptions of the missing books as thoroughly as I could. As I told you before, I would normally expect a copy or two of most of them to appear at this type of event. Everyone's books will be on display in their booths or at the special layout for the Friday auction. My plan is to wander through all of the displays and see if anything catches my attention."

"Won't that draw some attention to yourself?" asked Wilson.

"No, I don't think so. I'm a retired dealer who knows many of the other dealers. If I just say I am scouting for a longtime client it would seem credible."

"Will it be hard to inspect books if there are lots of people milling about?"

"I plan to do my first pass tomorrow afternoon when the dealers are setting up their booths. It's quite normal for dealers to visit each other's displays. It's a relatively quiet time. I have managed to get a pass into the set-up period; I called an old friend and volunteered to help him man his booth. His name is Colin Mackenzie from London, England."

"What will you do if you find a suspicious book?"

"I'll ask the dealer to hold it for me while I contact my client. Again, that's a quite normal thing to do. Then I'll call you and we can decide our next step."

Wilson then turned to Fleming and said, "That's where we may need your help."

Inspector Fleming nodded, and then asked, "Could your presence and attention raise any alarm bells with the dealer if it is a stolen book?"

"Our premise, and I think it's a good one, is that if such a book is here the dealer who currently has it will have no idea that it was stolen. The thieves will almost assuredly have sold it into the market, maybe through more than one transaction. I doubt the thieves would actually come to a public event with such books themselves. Our hope is that if we do find a book we can trace its origin back."

"Well, that's about it," summed up Wilson. "Shall we go to dinner and then maybe watch the fireworks when it gets dark? Apparently we can get a decent view of the show from the patio in the hotel's courtyard, complete with bar service."

29

Sasha also arrived in Ottawa on Wednesday, having driven his van full of books and display paraphernalia from Philadelphia. He thought it would be fun to see the fireworks that evening and to do a bit of touring around the city the next day before setting up at the book fair location. Ottawa was an attractive city with the many government buildings, museums and institutions enclosed by the Ottawa River and the Rideau Canal. The enormous limestone towers of the Parliament Buildings dominated the city center.

That evening he wandered the downtown street mall area and ate dinner at a small sidewalk café. He was intrigued by the mixed sounds of English and French being spoken everywhere. He knew Canada was officially bilingual and that the French-dominated province of Quebec was just across the Ottawa River, but the easy comingling of the two languages was new to him.

As scheduled, he arrived at the Ottawa Convention Centre just after noon the next day.

As he entered the large complex he first encountered the many displays that had been arranged in the large foyer, all fronted by a huge banner that proclaimed *"Welcome to the Franklin Festival of Arctic Celebrations."* They included a large display of Arctic artifacts related to the Franklin expedition; a Franklin historical display by the British Greenwich Maritime Museum; a general Arctic history display by the Canadian Champlain Society, which had been publishing Canadian history for over 100 years; books and ephemera displays by a number of institutions such as the National gallery, the Royal Ontario Museum and the University of Alberta; and many displays of maps which depicted the unfolding knowledge of North America from the 1500s to the early 1900s. There was even a very colorful display of paintings by famous Inuit artists. Sasha grimaced slightly when he saw the WHI display, knowing it had been the start of his recent problems.

He proceeded to a high-ceiling conference room to set up his booth. About 100 other dealers were doing the same thing.

The spaces were arranged along five parallel corridors with booths on each side. His boxes had been delivered to his site by the Convention Centre staff. He had a standard space, about ten feet square, where he set up his bookshelves on the sides and back and a display table up front. Some of the larger dealers had spaces twice as large, usually in prime spots at the entrance to a corridor.

Once the booths were essentially set up and organized, some dealers started to roam the aisles looking for items of interest in other dealers' booths. This was quite normal as dealers often specialized in limited areas and sometimes could find a bargain in some booth where the dealer was not a specialist in that area or did not have a customer base that would pay a premium for it. Such deals were also facilitated by the general rule that sales to another dealer would be at a twenty percent discount.

The dealers represented a wide range of size and geography. At the top were the big dealers who had interests in Arctic exploration along with many other things. These included Jeremy Boucher of Columbus, Ohio; Simon Katz of New York; Colin Mackenzie of London and Margaret Thomas of Los Angeles. The large Canadian dealers were definitely there, including Chester Chalk of Vancouver and Stuart Scott of Toronto. There were many smaller dealers as well, many of them from Southern Ontario and Quebec, who lived within a day's drive of Ottawa. At least a half-dozen major antique map dealers were also there, with their usual large and colorful maps hung on the booth side panels and laid out on wide tables.

Sasha didn't do much searching for books; he was more focused on the surroundings and the dynamics, trying to detect if anything unusual was happening. A few dealers stopped into his booth to check his books but only one bought anything, a book related to an early explorer in the St. Lawrence River area and down into New England. It was generally related to Eastern Canada, not the Arctic, but was not out of place at an Ottawa book fair.

He noted one slight anomaly, but it didn't seem significant. An older fellow wandered into his booth and quickly looked over his books. When asked if he was looking for anything in particular, a quite normal approach to a potential customer, he simply said he was looking for a couple of specific Arctic books. What was a bit unusual was that he didn't have the normal colorful dealer photo-identification badge hanging from his neck. That was the way the Fair security people could identify who could be in the area in off-hours, such as this setup time, and who could take books openly in and out of the fair. He said he came to fairs such as this to help other dealers, old friends. The plain badge hanging around his neck just said *"Advisor: Herb Trawets, California."* Sasha didn't think much more about it.

30

After Herb Trawets had completed his rounds of the book sellers' displays, he called Wilson and arranged to meet in their hotel lounge again.

When he got there he saw the two FBI agents but there was no sign of the RCMP Inspector.

"I have made a pass through the displays and must report that I didn't find anything very suspicious. Of the sixteen Arctic books on your list, there were copies of nine of them, more than I had expected. In fact, there were two or three copies of four of them. I was able to flip through them as I browsed the various offerings and I didn't see anything that would appear to link them to the stolen books. Even with the general descriptions I had, I can say that most of them can be definitely eliminated, as they were better copies than the ones that were stolen. And the others had nothing distinctive about them."

"I guess that's not surprising," said Wilson. "We knew it was a longshot but it was worth trying."

"Is there anything we can do?" asked Watkins.

"I will make another pass through the booths tomorrow in case I missed something or all the books weren't out on display yet, but that's not likely to change anything."

"I guess we can't just go around and ask everyone if they have bought any stolen books lately," joked Watkins.

"The problem is that in all likelihood by the time any of the books would get to these dealers they would have passed through others and look respectable."

"Then I guess we can't put up a sign saying 'Stolen Books Wanted' either," she said with a larger smile.

They just sat in silence for a few minutes, feeling somewhat dejected. Then Herb said, "Maybe we could."

"Could what?" asked Wilson.

"Order a stolen book."

"What!"

"Say we could identify a book that is very rare and let it be known that we want a copy. Then, if we know where one is, we could watch to see if it gets stolen."

"That sounds crazy and even more of a longshot than our coming here."

"Besides, how could we get involved in stealing a book?" interjected Watkins.

"I'm just thinking out loud. We would need to involve the owner of the target book, of course, and be sure we can identify it. Don't you guys use marked money when dealing with kidnappers or extortionists? It would be kind of the same thing."

"Right, we advertise that we want a specific copy of a rare book." Wilson added with a slight tone of sarcasm."

"Let me work on the idea overnight. We do know that books were stolen from the WHI. They do have rare books. We could involve them. In fact, when I was going to the booksellers' area today I noticed all of the various displays in the entrance foyer area of the Convention Centre. I did see a WHI display. It jumped out to me because of the connection to our search. We could approach them."

"OK, think about it some more but we won't go near the WHI area yet. Remember, someone there could be a thief."

BOOK FOUR

The Franklin Story

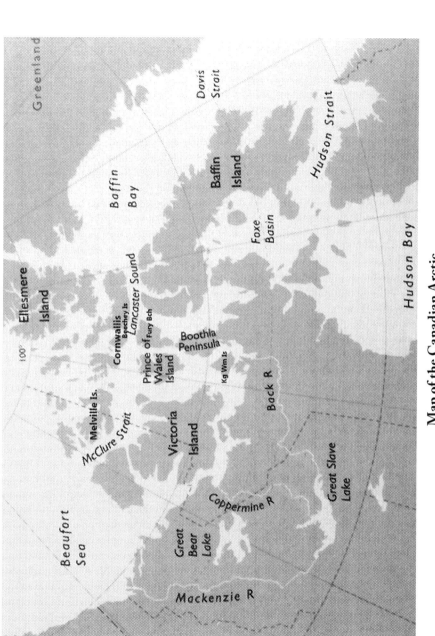

Map of the Canadian Arctic

31

October, 1845

Sir John Franklin was very pleased. Since leaving England the previous May, his two-ship expedition to the Arctic in search of a Northwest Passage to the Pacific Ocean had gone well.

They had sailed westward through the Lancaster Sound in the High Arctic and had circumnavigated Cornwallis island. He had hoped that there would be a passage north and west from that Island but had been turned back by the dense Arctic Ocean ice pack. Nevertheless, that was a new discovery.

Now they were set up to wait out the winter in a camp they had assembled on Beechey Island. All was well.

As usual, he assembled his officers for dinner in the main hut they had constructed. Seated at the head of the table, Franklin was flanked by his two most senior officers. Commander James Fitzjames was his senior officer on the ship HMS Erebus, the ship that Franklin sailed in. Captain Francis Crozier was the captain of the second ship, the HMS Terror. There were twenty-one other officers present. The total complement of the two ships was 129.

"Gentlemen," said Franklin, as the room became silent, "we have had a grand start to this mission. Our progress to this point has been exemplary. Although we were turned back by the ice north of Cornwallis Island, we have determined that a North-West Passage does not exist in that direction. When the ice clears next spring, we shall head west or south, depending on how the seas open up. Can we hear some brief reports on the status of our current situation?"

Commander Fitzjames spoke first. "Both ships are safely moored and secured for the winter. Their thick hulls with the steel sheathing will prevent any damage from the surrounding ice."

Captain Crozier added, "The provisions needed for the next nine months have been separated and assembled. We are ready for the winter."

Other officers gave brief reports about the camp that had been constructed, the preparation of the ice sledges that would be used for exploratory trips away from the camp, and the organization of the crews into groups responsible for various tasks.

Franklin spoke again. "Be sure everyone is kept busy. The winter will be long, and the weeks without the sun rising over the horizon can be tedious. Activity is the cure for isolation and boredom."

Someone spoke up. "We have already organized groups for sledge training, general education sessions and entertainment. After all, we have one thousand books and many musical instruments on board."

Another voice said, "And lots of wine, ale and tobacco!"

With that, Franklin said, "Time for dinner to be served. But first, lift your glasses in a toast: To the Queen!"

"To the Queen," replied everyone as a chorus.

October, 1846

John Franklin was generally pleased with the state of the expedition, although he had hoped they would have made even greater progress over the past summer.

By late June, the ice had started to open and the crews had prepared the ships for sailing. Shrouding was removed, masts were restored and materials were stowed.

The only setback over the previous winter was that three crew members had died. That had been unexpected since they had ample provisions. However, they had wasted away and had great difficulty breathing. The ships' surgeons attributed it to consumption, which they probably had contracted before the expedition began.

To Franklin's delight, the passage to the south of Lancaster Sound became passable. That had been the primary hope for the expedition, as expressed in his orders from the British Admiralty.

It had been a hard journey over three months, as the crews needed to constantly chop channels in the ice and manually drag the ships through openings. The ice was melting and thinning, but it was always present.

By the end of the summer season, they had progressed south down a long channel and had reached the northern shores of King William Land.

As the ice froze around the ships, they had been prepared for the winter, with shrouding and snow banking to provide insulation. The ships would be their base camp for the next nine months. Since they did have steam boilers and coal supplies on board, warmth and fresh water would not be a problem.

Franklin huddled with Commander Fitzjames and Captain Crozier over his maps and charts laid out on the table in his room at the back of the Erebus. There was no map of their specific location; no European had been here before.

Franklin summarized their situation. "We know where we are geographically from our celestial and solar observations; essentially 69° 50' North Latitude and 98° 40' West Longitude. This means that the land we see to the south-east is undoubtedly King William Land and that the continental mainland is not much more than one hundred miles south of here. Back's Great

Fish River will be there. One more summer season should get us there and allow us to follow the continental coastline westward to Bering's Strait and the Pacific."

Fitzjames said, "Even if it takes two more summers, we can make it. Our provisions can be stretched well into 1848."

Crozier added, "And, as we move south there should be more vegetation and wildlife to sustain us."

"There sure isn't anything up here," said Fitzjames.

"Right. The few small bands of natives we spot don't seem to have much, even for themselves. I don't know how they manage to survive."

"Well, gentlemen," said Franklin. "Let's be sure everything is organized for the long winter coming upon us. Last winter was handled well, but fatigue and isolation can work away at everyone. I sense some lethargy setting in. We had known that the journey could take three years or more, but had hoped it would be two. Time will now move more slowly."

June, 1847

Sir John Franklin was contemplating his situation.

They had been away from England for over two years now. The past winter had been harsh and there was no sign of the sea ice opening yet, but that should start soon.

There had been a few more deaths over the winter. Consumption was a factor as was scurvy, which surprised him. Their rations of lemon juice were supposed to prevent that. Fatigue and lethargy were affecting many.

His aspirations for the coming summer were high. Surely they would break out of the northern ice and return to England in glory.

He was 61 years old. Certainly he was famous, but that was for his Arctic overland excursions which occurred over twenty years ago. He also knew that he was really more famous for surviving, not discovering much. He was "The Man Who Ate His Boots."

The last two decades had been without glory. First the doldrums of a navy career in peace and then a disastrous assignment as the Governor of Van Diemen's Land in the South Pacific. This current expedition was going to secure his name in history.

At dinner with his senior officers there was an improved tone of anticipation. The days were getting longer and the weather was improving.

Something was bothering Franklin, but he couldn't decide what it was. Indigestion perhaps.

Sir John Franklin died on June 11, 1847.

Ship Trapped in Arctic Ice

April, 1848

Captain Crozier and Commander Fitzjames huddled on the shore of King William Land. Francis Crozier had assumed overall command of the expedition when John Franklin had died almost a year earlier.

The past year had been very difficult.

The ice did not open up at all in the summer of 1847. They were in the same area that they had reached in the fall of 1846. They had only slowly drifted south with the ice pack last summer. Now, in fact, they had just abandoned the ships and moved the crew and provisions to land.

There were now 105 out of the original 129 people who had started on the journey three years earlier. Many of them were sick and weak. Provisions were running low. Vegetation was essentially non-existent on the barren, rocky land and they had no skills in fishing through ice or hunting polar bears or whales.

Captain Crozier said, "We must do something to get help. We will be lucky if many of us survive this summer, even with reduced rations, and next winter will be impossible. If the ice holds fast again, no one will find us, even if they are looking. And that's not likely as we have only been gone for three years. We were expected to be gone this long."

Commander Fitzjames asked, "What are our options?"

"We could send a party back north overland to Lancaster Sound, but not likely to Beechey Island, as the Sound will definitely be open water in the summer. Even if a ship arrives in the area before the end of summer, a long shot, it would be difficult to make contact. And then for them to return here overland with supplies and remove us to safety before winter is unlikely."

"Perhaps even a party of two or three could try that."

"Such a small party couldn't even take enough provisions to sustain themselves for the trip. A larger party with a sledge would be necessary."

"What else, then?"

"There is a cache of supplies at Fury Beach on the east coast of Somerset Island. Again a party might get there, but couldn't bring back enough supplies for over 100 people to survive another winter. It's the same longshot hope that there might be a ship there to connect with that could send a rescue mission."

"What if we try to move everyone there?"

"There would be provisions for a while but we would be totally depending on the arrival of a rescue ship before we perished."

"So, what else is there to do?"

"The other possibility is to move south over the ice to the mainland shore near Back's Great Fish River We know people have been there before and we know there are trading posts inland with people and supplies."

Franklin's Fate

"*The stories of those explorers say the route up that river is very difficult and those trading posts are a long way inland.*"

"*I know. But, it's the only place where we know there will actually be people and supplies. Even if some of us make it we can get help. They are experienced with the north. They can marshal resources to come for us. As well, we will more likely find food to survive on the journey going south rather than farther north into the Arctic wilderness.*"

"*It seems unlikely to succeed.*"

"*All of our options seem like that. We need to do something.*"

"*Alright. I'll round up those that appear strong enough to go.*"

"*Where is that piece of paper we have made some notes on? I'll add a brief update of our current situation.*"

Over the next couple of weeks the bedraggled group advanced south, reaching the mainland near the mouth of Back's Great Fish River. Many of them fell by the wayside and died.

The few that did reach that first destination realized that it was impossible for them to continue on the arduous journey inland. They turned back north, heading for their base camp near the abandoned ships. Their only chance was that a rescue party would arrive before their supplies ran out.

Very few made it back. No rescue party ever arrived.

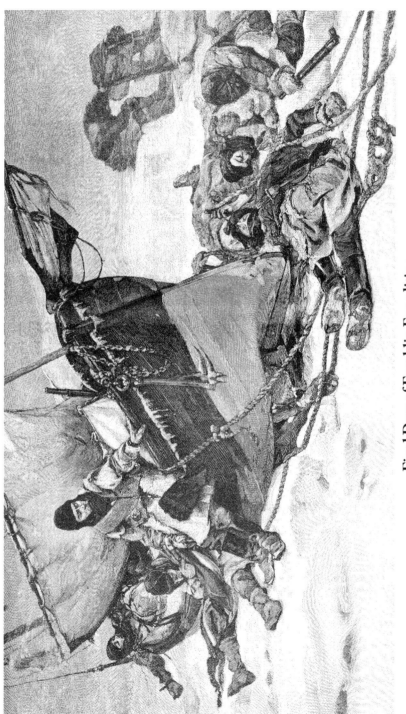

Final Days of Franklin Expedition

32

It was now late Thursday afternoon in Ottawa. The booksellers had completed their set-ups and were mingling about, renewing acquaintances and chatting about their expectations for the fair. They were anticipating the Gala Reception that was going to take place that evening in the large ballroom that was part of the Convention Centre. That was going to be preceded by a presentation about John Franklin in an adjoining arts theater. Attendance was expected to be large as it was of interest to everyone who was involved with the Festival, not just the book events. In fact, the whole evening was going to be a major event for the Ottawa social leaders, whether government, cultural, educational or business related.

By 6:00 pm the venue was full. Notably seated in the center of the front row was the Prime Minister of Canada, Robert Durocher.

Pierre Clarke, the Minister of Canadian Heritage in the federal cabinet, strode onto the stage.

"Welcome, Bienvenue to this evening's special activities in support of *The Franklin Festival of Arctic Celebrations*. This week-long event is enabling us to focus on our Arctic heritage and to remember the history of its discovery and development. I am sure that everyone has noticed the many displays in the foyer of the Convention Centre that capture so much of that history and of the more recent successful ventures that discovered Franklin's long-lost ships. I hope you will take the time to visit them.

"Later this evening we will all be gathering in the main ballroom for the gala reception, where we can mix and mingle and share stories and experiences related to the north. I am sure there will be some fascinating tales.

"First, however, we are going to be educated and entertained with the real story of Sir John Franklin and his legendary, but tragic voyage of discovery into the Arctic one hundred and seventy-five years ago.

"To give us that information, I am pleased to introduce Dr. Jonathan Robertson, Professor of History and Geography at the University of British Columbia and a recognized expert on the early voyages of exploration to Canada's west and north.

"Dr. Robertson, please join us."

Franklin's Fate

"Thank you, Minister. Mr. Prime Minister, ladies and gentlemen, it's a great pleasure to join you this evening in celebration of the discovery of Sir John Franklin's lost ships.

"In a few minutes I will share with you the story of John Franklin – his fame, his fortune, his follies and his fate.

"But first, let's acknow-ledge the admirable efforts over the past ten years that led to the discovery of the two ships, the *Terror* and the *Erebus*, that brought the Franklin expedition to our Arctic waters almost two centuries ago and have been missing ever since.

"People had searched for the ships many times without success. In 2008, a renewed search was started using modern technologies such as side-scanning sonar. It was tedious work since sea conditions are suitable for less than two months a year and ice pack movements often dictated where the search could be done each year.

"The search had been stimulated by private groups such as the Arctic Research Foundation and the Royal Canadian Geographic Society. It had been supported by the Canadian government and the Nunavut Territorial government. It involved resources from the Canadian Coast Guard, the Canadian Hydrographic Service, The Canadian Navy, and Parks Canada, plus others.

"For six years they searched in vain. The conditions were often difficult and many times the searches were frustrated by the elements. Then, in 2014, forced to operate in a secondary area due to the sea-ice problems, they discovered the hulk of Franklin's ship, the *Erebus*. It was in 11 meters of water and in remarkably good shape. Over the next two seasons expert divers scanned the wreck and retrieved many artifacts, some of which are on display in the exhibits at this event.

"Then, in 2016, again diverted by ice, the wreck of the second ship, the *Terror*, was discovered in the same general region, this time in 48 meters of water. I will acknowledge that the exact locations of the ships has not been revealed, to minimize the possibility of trespass and vandalism on these National Historic Sites.

"It was a remarkable achievement, and one we are now celebrating.

"As I now move on to relate the tale of John Franklin and his Arctic expedition, I will bridge to it with two observations. The remnants of the Franklin expedition were found exactly where Franklin planned to go. But no one looked for him there, as literally dozens of ships tried to find him.

Franklin's Fate

"The ships have now been found where the folklore tales of the northern Inuit people had said they were. It took some fortuitous events to actually search there.

"Sometimes the power of science and authority needs to learn from the wisdom of practical knowledge and experience.

"And therein lies the story of the tragic fate of Franklin as well."

33

"John Franklin is certainly a famous British explorer; look at how we are celebrating him today.

"What is he famous for? Leading an expedition to the Arctic where he and his 128 crew members died.

"Why did he become famous? Because no one knew where he had actually gone and whether the crew members were alive for many years. The 'Search for Franklin' consumed his nation, and much of the world, for many years. In fact, here we are today, 175 years later, still looking for clues about their actual fate.

"Let's start at the beginning. John Franklin was born in 1786, one of nine children of an English merchant. By the age of 14 he had joined the British navy. Over the next 15 years he served on many ships and rose in the ranks. He gained great experience: he was at the Battle of Copenhagen with Nelson (1800), sailed with Flinders to Australia (1801), was at the Battle of the South China Sea (1804), in the Battle of Trafalgar against Napoleon (1805) and at the Battle of New Orleans (1815).

"His first Arctic experience was as commander of the ship *Trent*, part of Buchan's expedition that tried to go to the North Pole via Spitzbergen in 1818. They made little real progress against the ice, but did reach about 80 Degrees North, a notable achievement for the times.

"John Barrow, Secretary of the Admiralty, was determined to find a Northwest Passage across the Arctic Ocean north of Canada. Two hundred years earlier, in the 1600s, attempts to find such a passage out of Hudson Bay had been attempted by Henry Hudson, Thomas James, Luke Foxe and others. Once that was proven to be impossible, exploration essentially stopped. The farther north routes seemed too daunting.

"In the late 1700s Samuel Hearne and Alexander Mackenzie did travel overland to reach the shore of the Arctic Ocean via the Coppermine and Mackenzie Rivers respectively, but there had been no follow-up. Thus, for almost two hundred years sea-based northern activity was limited to whaling and fur trading.

"In 1819 Barrow decided to renew the search for a passage. He sent William Parry to sail into the Arctic Archipelago. Parry made amazing progress westward through Lancaster Sound all the way to Melville Island, an achievement that would not be bettered for many decades.

"At the same time he sent an overland expedition through central Canada to the Arctic shores, looking for evidence of navigable waters. John Franklin was put in charge of that expedition.

"On the surface, the expedition did reach the Arctic shore via the Coppermine River and did survey hundreds of miles of new territory.

"In reality the expedition was one disaster after another. Planned provisions from the Hudson's Bay Company never materialized. The only guides used were two natives and two fur traders who were quite unreliable. No one in the British contingent had any experience travelling and surviving in the harsh Arctic environment; they were navy people after all. People died of starvation and scurvy. Two people were murdered. Some of the party undeniably committed cannibalism.

"While a couple of people went to look for help and supplies, the rest hunkered down in a make-shift camp. By the end, just before the rescue party did return, the survivors were resorting to eating lichen off the rocks and chewing their leather boots for nutrition. Only 11 of the 22 members of the expedition survived.

"Nevertheless, John Franklin returned home in 1822 as a successful explorer and became a legend as 'The Man Who Ate His Boots.' His published journals became popular reading for the English establishment.

"Three years later, in 1825, John Franklin was again sent to lead an overland expedition to the Arctic shores. This time he reached the Arctic via the Mackenzie River. He surveyed the shoreline westward into Alaska and his companions surveyed east to The Coppermine River. They had filled in much of the unknown territory. Only a few hundred miles from the end of Franklin's first expedition to Back's Great Fish River were uncharted and the presumption was that the Arctic shore line would continue along that stretch. The Northwest Passage, although unnavigable due to ice, had almost been found.

"In 1827 Franklin returned home again as a successful explorer. Two years later he was knighted for his successes. Now Sir John Franklin, he was ready for new challenges.

"However, times were slow for naval officers. There were no wars to fight or new explorations to undertake. Much of the expanding world was being defined by the traders of the East India Company, The Hudson's Bay Company, and various ventures into Africa. Naval officers were often furloughed and placed on half-pay.

"Franklin's next opportunity was being appointed Governor of Van Diemen's Land, now known as Tasmania, in 1837. This large island off the south of Australia was essentially a penal colony. It was administered by displaced Englishmen, often third or fourth sons of gentry or adventurers looking for a life free from England. They had established their own society, habits and hierarchies. They had no time for a 50-year-old mainline navy officer who wanted to bring new administrative processes and disciplines to their world. Franklin had no skills in diplomacy or politics.

"It was a disaster. In fact, when Franklin decided to fire some of the key administrators they appealed to the government officials in England and Franklin was called back to England rather unceremoniously in 1843.

"However fate was to intervene. John Barrow was again organizing an Arctic expedition to find the last link in a Northwest Passage. Many of the experienced Arctic explorers were too old or reluctant to lead the effort. John Franklin was available and eager to do it, even if he was 59 years old when they set sail in 1845.

"The expedition was well organized. Two sturdy ships with Arctic experience, the *Erebus* and the *Terror*, were fitted with iron sheathing and had steam engines installed that could drive propellers that were protected from the ice. Although limited in their actual power and by the coal capacity of the ships, they added a totally new aspect to Arctic sailing.

"Provisions for three years of isolation in the Arctic for the complement of 129 men were stored, considered ample for the venture. The numbers were staggering: 100,000 pounds of meat; 135,000 pounds of flour; 35,000 pounds of biscuits; 20,000 pints of soup; plus vegetables and condiments. There were also 4,000 gallons of liquor, 5,000 gallons of ale, and ample wine for the officers.

"1000 books, notepaper and an organ were available to help pass the long dark winters of isolation that were expected.

"They set sail in May 1845. Franklin's orders were straightforward. Sail west through Lancaster Sound as far as Cornwallis Island and then search for the best opening in the sea ice to find the last link in the Northwest Passage. If the sea was open to the south, that was the preferred choice. If not, try to go north into the open sea beyond the island archipelago.

"The early stages of the journey were successful. After minor delays, they did traverse Lancaster Sound and reach Cornwallis Island. The seas to the south were ice-filled but the channel north was passable. Although they were eventually turned back by the polar ice, they did circumnavigate Cornwallis Island, a new achievement.

"They wintered on Beechey Island, on the north side of Lancaster Sound. This was the same area that Parry had reached over a quarter century earlier. Although three men did die during the winter and were buried there, spirits would have been generally high. They had already achieved some success.

"In the summer of 1846, the ice was opening up again. What we now know is that the channel south into Victoria Straight became passable, because that is where Franklin sailed. One mystery is why Franklin didn't leave a message in a cairn on Beechey Island saying which direction he was going. That would have been normal and expected. If he had done so, at least some of the crew might have been rescued by the later search parties.

"So, fortune was with them and they sailed south. In retrospect, it was bad fortune. The ice in the path to Victoria Straight was never seen to be open again for many decades. There was even a secondary piece of bad luck. When the ships approached the north end of King William Island they veered westward down the Straight. That was natural since they were trying to find a passage to the west. In fact that channel was a particularly bad area for ice blockages. The channel to the east of the island opened up more readily. They didn't know that, of course, and may also have thought that it wasn't really a channel since King William Land hadn't been identified as an island yet.

"When the winter of 1846 set in, the ships were icebound in Victoria Straight. Again, all was well. They had made good progress. They had provisions. Surely they would break through in the next summer. Franklin would have known their geographic location from observations of the sun and stars and would have realized that he was only a few hundred miles from the point he had reached overland in 1820.

"At the end of the Arctic winter, waiting for the ice to open, on June 11, 1847, John Franklin died. The information was written on the one piece of paper that has ever been discovered from the Franklin expedition, found in a cairn on King William Island. It is factual with no explanation. His body has never been discovered; he was likely buried at sea through a hole cut in the ice, but a land based burial was possible. People still search.

"He was 61 years old, not young for those times. Tuberculosis was possible. Weakness due to scurvy setting in was possible, as the lemon juice the ship carried was now over two years old and likely ineffective. Many of the ships' provisions had been supplied in tins, which were later shown to have faulty lead soldering and which could have added the effects of lead poisoning. We will never know the total answer.

Franklin's Fate

"The leadership of the expedition now passed to Francis Crozier, Captain of the *Terror*, assisted by James Fitzjames, now Captain of the *Erebus*. They were both seasoned officers.

"1847 passed with no break in the ice.

"The spring of 1848 arrived and things were now getting desperate. At least 25 people had died. Provisions were running short. Scurvy was rampant.

"In April 1848 they organized an attempt to send a group to the mainland near Back's Great Fish River and to journey hundreds of miles inland to the far-off trading posts of the Hudson's Bay Company. The trip would prove to be impossible for the men in the shape they were in. The river is a treacherous route, with over 80 rapids and falls, through a barren land with little plant or animal life.

"They barely made it to the mainland. Most of the excursion died. A few returned to the ships.

"The ultimate irony is that those desperate, bedraggled members of the Franklin expedition that went to the mouth of Back's Great Fish River actually closed the link on the discovery of a Northwest Passage. Neither they nor anyone else knew that at the time.

"Although it's possible that a few people survived a bit longer, it is likely that almost everyone from the Franklin Expedition died by the end of 1848. The last survivors probably died of starvation; signs of some cannibalism emerged when the location of the lost expedition was eventually found. However, most of the people died before the food was exhausted. Modern analyses have indicated that tuberculosis, which brings on Addison's disease, which causes dehydration, weight loss and weakness was likely a significant factor. Scurvy, lead effects, botulism and just general exposure to the harsh environment undoubtedly all contributed to the deaths.

"To this day there are many questions about their fate.

"Why didn't they try to get to safety sooner? Probably because through 1847 they thought they were alright and that the ice would open again the next year to allow them to pass on. Multi-year isolation in the Arctic had happened to many other exploration ventures.

"When they did try to leave, why did they go south to the inhospitable Back's Fish River area? Even in good shape, that would have been a formidable route. Why not head north, where the terrain was better, where caches of food existed, and rescue vessels could be expected? This is unknown. Perhaps they doubted that rescue operations would be underway. Perhaps the mental deterioration due to scurvy and lead poisoning partially explains it. Perhaps the leaders who had that knowledge were no longer functioning.

"Why didn't they do better foraging off the land? Surely animals, fish and whales existed? Yes, those sources did exist but they were scarce and hard to get. King William Island is especially barren. Besides, no one on the expedition really knew how to hunt or fish. Seriously. They were navy men. They didn't even have rifles. They had no skills in living off the land and had not brought anyone with them that did know. The previous overland expeditions of Franklin and others had been supported by native and Metis guides; no one like that was on the ships.

"Why didn't they ask for and get more help from the Inuit natives? This answer is more complicated. To start with, the British considered the Inuit to be uneducated savages and unworthy of help or trust. The fact that they survived in those harsh conditions did not seem to impress the navy men. They did not even have a translator with them. Remember, this was the era of displacing and annihilating native groups in America and Australia and of enslaving natives in Africa.

"Arrogance bred ignorance.

"Besides, the Inuit would have been of limited help for their survival. They lived and travelled in relatively small family groups. They were nomads who hunted and fished. Only a few thousand Inuit inhabited the whole span of the Arctic islands. They did not have villages. Their own survival was often perilous. A small band of Inuit could not have supplied or supported a flotilla of 128 men.

"Again, remember the times. The Arctic was generally claimed by the British because of the explorers who had ventured there, but no attempt at settlement was made. Canada did not exist as a nation yet. When Canada did start to pay attention to the north it was seventy-five years later, in the 1920s and 1930s, with the establishment of a few RCMP detachments and a few trading posts. Villages didn't grow up until the 1950s with the Canadian and United States military presence due to the Cold War with Russia and the building of the Defense Early Warning radar system.

"Even today, there are likely less than 20,000 Inuit in the High Arctic and most of the villages spread out over that large area have populations of a few hundred, perhaps two thousand in the larger ones.

"Why didn't the many rescue voyages find and save the Franklin expedition?

"The simple answer is that they didn't start looking until it was too late and they didn't look in the right place.

Franklin's Fate

"To start with, the British Admiralty didn't consider the Franklin Expedition as being missing until 1848. After all, they had provisions for three years and were experienced Arctic explorers.

"The government was very distracted. In 1848 there were revolutions in essentially every European country. Monarchies and establishments were being overthrown. Populism was on the rise. Even in Britain, which was arguably the most liberal European nation, there were major protests demanding political reform. Only men who owned land could vote; the people were demanding more rights and participation in government.

"Urged on by John Franklin's wife and some sympathizers within the exploration community, there was a building public demand for some action. Finally, the government did start organizing rescue missions in 1848. In fact, over the next five years there were dozens of Arctic 'Search for Franklin' voyages. At least three-dozen expeditions took place. However, some of those had multiple ships in them, which often separated to check out different areas. Over four dozen ships were involved in total.

"As a result the High Arctic was thoroughly mapped and a more northerly Northwest Passage was discovered by Robert McClure, although that just meant that he found an impenetrable ice path between the many islands. The final hundreds of miles of the path were discovered by sledge travel, not by his ships, which he had abandoned in the ice flows.

"The published journals of those many expeditions fascinated the public back in Britain. Today, they form the cornerstone items in any book collection related to Arctic exploration. I know you will see many of those publications at the antiquarian book fair that is being held over the next two days and at the rare book auction on Friday. Be sure to check out those events.

"However, those explorers didn't find the Franklin expedition or its remnants. They never looked down the channel where Franklin went. The ice never opened up in that direction again and Franklin had not left any indication of where he had gone. Any Inuit natives that they did encounter in the higher latitudes were too far removed from the pertinent area and could not provide any reliable information.

"In 1854, almost ten years after the Franklin Expedition had sailed, John Rae, a Hudson's Bay Company explorer was mapping the Arctic shores around the Boothia Peninsula. He was not looking for Franklin. He encountered a group of Inuit who told him tales of many dead sailors from two ships who had been stranded years earlier in the region of King William Island. They had many artifacts that could only have come from the Franklin expedition: medals, clothing, buttons, implements, etc. It was too late in the season for Rae to get to that location and so he returned to England with the news.

"John Rae was a renowned Arctic explorer. His untiring journeys and major geographic mappings were legendary. He was considered a bit of an outsider as he was a private individual, not military, and had adopted the native style of clothing (furs, not cloth), land travel (dog sleds, not man-haul heavy sleds), river travel (canoes, not heavy boats) and building (igloos, not tents).

"He had led a couple of overland excursions looking for Franklin five years earlier. He was not successful, but in hindsight probably came closer to finding him than anyone.

"Although Rae's news was not unexpected, it was still disturbing to the British establishment and the public. He was criticized for not following up immediately on the information and going to the locations. When he reported the Inuit statements that some of the sailors had resorted to cannibalism, he was ostracized. Such a thing was unfathomable, and it was probably just lies spread by the savages who had probably killed the sailors people said. British hypocrisy and indignity was at its peak.

"They did know how to shoot the messenger though. It is worth noting that of all the many explorers who led significant excursions to the Arctic in search of Franklin and the Northwest Passage, only John Rae never received a knighthood.

"The narrow thinking was further emphasized by the Admiralty's decision that the Franklin search was now complete. The reward for the discovery was given to Rae, and no follow-up expeditions were planned.

"A navigable Northwest Passage did not exist and the Suez Canal was on the horizon as a short route to Asia. As well, a war was being fought in the Crimea; resources could not be wasted on more Arctic ventures.

"John Franklin's wife was outraged. Certainly there had to be a follow-up expedition to confirm Rae's story and to learn more about what had actually happened to her husband and his expedition. But, the authorities did not budge.

"Four years later, Lady Jane Franklin commissioned Captain Francis McClintock to sail to the region in question and to find out what had really happened. He sailed in 1858 and by the summer of 1859 had discovered the area along King William Island where the tragedies had occurred. There were bodies, artifacts, abandoned sledges and long boats. McClintock was also able to buy some remnants from local Inuit who had scavenged the area over the years.

DISCOVERY OF THE CAIRN CONTAINING SIR JOHN FRANKLIN'S PAPERS.

Discovery of Cairn on King William Is.

Franklin's Fate

In one cairn was a single page of paper with brief notes that had been made over two years. It's the only written record that has been found. It confirmed the wintering at Beechey Island in the winter of 1845-46, the date of Franklin's death in 1847, some of the expedition's logistics, and the plans for the last desperate attempt to escape the north via Back's Great Fish River in 1848. This piece of paper is as much a mystery as a help. Why did they record events spread over more than two years on this one sloppily written paper? They had elaborate writing supplies on the ships, let alone log books and diaries. Why was this the only paper left in the cairn? Why hadn't they left more records and messages? We don't know.

"Over the years, more artifacts have been found and tales from the Inuit have added to the knowledge of the Franklin Expedition's final days. But there are still many unanswered questions.

"The location of the ships was perhaps the last great mystery. Now that has been solved. They were encased in the ice of Victoria Straight for years, drifting south with the ice pack, until finally being released to sink in the waters south of King William Island.

"Thus ends my abbreviated story of the great tragedy of the Franklin Expedition. It could have been avoided.

"The British newspaper *The Guardian* perhaps summarized it best. 'Eyewitness descriptions of starving, exhausted men staggering through the snow without condescending to ask local people how they survived in such a wilderness' is the enduring image of the lost Franklin expedition.

"Thank you for your attention. Let's go and join the Gala celebration."

Sole Surviving Document

H. M. S.hips *Erebus and Terror* ...

{ Wintered in the Ice in

28 of May 184 7 { Lat. 70° 5' N Long. 98° 23' W

Having wintered in 1846—7 at Beechey Island

in Lat 74° 43' 28" N. Long 91° 39' 15" W after having

ascended Wellington Channel to Lat 77° and returned

by the West side of Cornwallis Island

Sir John Franklin commanding the Expedition

All well

Commander.

WHOEVER finds this paper is requested to forward it to the Secretary of the Admiralty, London, *with a note of the time and place at which it was found*: or, if more convenient, to deliver it for that purpose to the British Consul at the nearest Port.

QUINCONQUE trouvera ce papier est prié d'y marquer le tems et lieu ou il l'aura trouvé, et de le faire parvenir au plutot au Secretaire de l'Amirauté Britannique à Londres.

CUALQUIERA que hallare este Papel, se le suplica de enviarlo al Secretario del Almirantazgo, en Londrés, con una nota del tiempo y del lugar en donde se halló.

EEN ieder die dit Papier mogt vinden, wordt hiermede verzogt, om het zelve, ten spoedigste, te willen zenden aan den Heer Minister van de Marine der Nederlanden in 's Gravenhage, of wel aan den Secretaris der Britsche Admiraliteit, te London, en daar by te voegen eene Nota, inhoudende de tyd en de plaats alwaar dit Papier is gevonden geworden

FINDEREN af dette Papiir ombedes, naar Leilighed gives, at sende samme til Admiralitets Secretairen i London, eller nærmeste Embedsmand i Danmark, Norge, eller Sverrig. Tiden og Stœdit hvor dette er fundet ønskes venskabeligt paategnet.

WER diesen Zettel findet, wird hier-durch ersucht denselben an den Secretair des Admiralitets in London einzusenden, mit gefälliger angabe an welchen ort und zu welcher zeit er gefunden worden ist.

Party consisting of 2 Officers and 6 Men

left the Ships on Monday 24th May 1847

BOOK FIVE

The Pursuit

34

The large gathering in the theater filed out and headed for the ballroom. Chatter was high; people were both commenting upon the presentation they had just heard and greeting acquaintances they spotted in the crowd.

In the ballroom the walls were decorated with large reproductions of photos and maps related to the Arctic in general and the Franklin Expedition in particular. People tended to look at them in more detail than they would have before, given the speech.

Bars and food stations were spread throughout the large space. Tables, both high stand-up ones and lower regular ones were spread out along the walls where people could pause to set their drinks or eat a few appetizers from their plates. The setup was designed to encourage mixing and wandering.

An observer would notice trends in the people patterns.

The Prime Minister didn't stay long. He didn't get any food or drinks. People who were senior enough or were comfortable with him would chat with him briefly and move on. This wasn't a place to take much of his time.

Other government ministers stayed longer, ate and drank, and held longer conversations, although they were careful to generally keep moving to work the room.

Business and cultural leaders tended to make cursory stops to chat with the government leaders and then congregate with their own groups.

This was the Ottawa social scene in action.

Outsiders, such as tourists who had bought tickets to the event, tended to mingle little and watch from the sidelines.

Of course there were a few outsiders who made a point of greeting everyone who seemed important, especially the politicians, so they could tell their friends back home how they met with the celebrities. They were politely tolerated.

The dealers from the book fair were more like the outsiders, but with little or no interest in the Ottawa social dynamics. The ones that knew each other relatively well soon congregated in one place, drinks in hand.

Simon Katz was chatting with Margaret Thomas and Jeremy Boucher.

"Fascinating presentation, in a way. We all deal in Arctic books, and particularly in the many journals of exploration related to the search for Franklin. I'm not sure I actually paid that much attention to the real Franklin story before."

"I agree, Simon," said Margaret. "The exploits and travails of the searchers created many of the collectible books about Arctic history. As the professor said, there were dozens of expeditions."

"Professor Robertson certainly took some of the glamour off the legend of John Franklin. I remember he did the same thing about George Vancouver at that big auction in Vancouver a couple of years ago."

"It's like Mark Antony was wrong with his eulogy to Julius Caesar. He said, 'The evil that men do lives after them; the good is oft interred with their bones.' It seems that people like Franklin and Vancouver have had their good deeds remembered and their shortcomings forgotten."

"There is always the axiom that the winners and the survivors get to write the history books."

"I wonder how much action we'll see at the book fair tomorrow," inserted Jeremy, changing the topic. "I hope this evening sparked some interest."

"You know," said Simon, "This reception is noisy and I really don't know anyone here. There is a quiet lounge downstairs. Do you want to bail out?"

They both nodded.

As they headed to the door they saw the two Canadian dealers, Chester Chalk and Stuart Scott, chatting in a corner.

"Hey, guys," said Margaret, "we're going down to a quieter spot. Want to join us?"

"Sure."

Then Margaret spotted Herb Trawets and Colin Mackenzie. They also joined in.

Once settled and with drinks on order, Jeremy spoke up. "Stuart, you are the closest to a local here. What's your take on tomorrow's fair and the auction?"

"Well, it should be OK. There are many wealthy people in this area and history is a topic of interest to many of them. There are a few good bookdealers here, but they're limited in scope. I suspect we'll see some curious people."

"You never know when you'll meet a new person that turns into a long-term customer," added Chester.

"Looking around the table, you have to wonder if it was a worthwhile trip for all of us," said Simon.

"Treat it like a vacation," said Margaret. "Something like the Seattle fair. It's not New York or L.A."

Jeremy laughed. "I guess we'll all be checking out the bidders at the auction, trying to find a real player. It's not as if we're going to find any key books in the auction since we are supplying them."

"Like the game of hide-and-seek," said Colin with his English accent and a twinkle in his eye.

There was a pause in the conversation as their drinks were delivered. Simon spoke up next.

"Have any of you had any visits from the authorities about stolen books?"

After a very long, quiet pause, Jeremy said, "What are you talking about?"

"Well you all know about that major theft of books from the Carnegie. Hundreds of valuable books missing and very few have turned up."

"What authorities are you talking about?" asked Margaret.

"I had a visit from the FBI some time ago. It was very general but I have to assume they're investigating all of that."

"Don't you think that was an isolated incident?" asked Chester. "The checks and controls there seemed unusually lax."

"Maybe," said Simon.

"I worry more about people stealing from me, both in my shop and in the booths at fairs. Even if you're diligent, people can go undetected," said Stuart.

"What are you concerned about, Simon?" asked Margaret.

"It's not so much a specific concern as it is a general thought. How are we preventing stolen books from getting into our systems?"

"We usually know something about the provenance of our books," said Colin.

"Usually, but not always. Buying books at auction or at fairs just gives you one level of provenance. How often do you go deeper? Look at the book that tripped the Carnegie guys up. The original crooked dealer sold it to another dealer at a fair, who in turn sold it to another dealer, who then syndicated it with two other dealers to market it. Those latter dealers were all credible and I know I could easily buy a book from them and sell it to a customer in good faith."

"That's the conundrum, isn't it," said Margaret. "Books don't have serial numbers and dealings often go through many hands. We are a business built on good faith."

"I know all that and I don't have any real solutions. But if I was candid, I would bet that at least some of us have handled a book that was stolen from Carnegie."

Again silence.

"Well, I guess I need another drink," said Chester.

Everyone laughed.

Herb Trawets hadn't said a word through that whole conversation.

35

Herb Trawets met up with the FBI agents again over breakfast the next morning.

"I did a lot more thinking and research about my idea last evening. The more I thought about it, the more of a wild idea it seems alright. But, what do we have to lose? The setup would be simple. I would just spread the word that I'm looking for a particular book or books and we would wait and watch to see if anything happens."

"Did you figure out a target book?"

"I think so. The WHI collection is listed on their website for researchers to browse. It doesn't have detailed descriptions but I know most of the relevant books and I knew what I was looking for: something rare and valuable and small. Remember only octavo or smaller-size books were stolen.

"The WHI has a copy of the Luke Foxe journal about his exploration into Hudson's Bay in the 1600s. It's a natural companion to the Thomas James journal of the same time. Remember, the James was on the list of stolen books from the WHI. In fact, it's a bit of a mystery to me why anyone would have stolen the James and not also have taken the Foxe. They are definitely both valuable and rare. For example, there is not a copy of either one here at the Ottawa fair."

Wilson then said, "Well, if we're going to try this we need to talk to Dr. Wright, the Director of Rare Books at the WHI. I'm sure she is here with the display. However, we shouldn't approach her there. She likely has other people with her and we could be recognized from our visits to the WHI. We interviewed a bunch of people. I have her phone number in my system. I'll call her and arrange a meeting."

Rhonda Wright was at the WHI display in the entrance of the Convention Centre. It was 9:00 a.m. and the doors were about to open. She had come to Ottawa with the display, accompanied by one of her curators, Dennis Davis. He had wandered down to the book fair area, out of curiosity. It was just opening as well. Rhonda didn't mind as she knew that it was likely going to be quiet in the early hours, as had happened the day before.

She was thinking about her decision to come to Ottawa. She had thought it would provide some exposure for WHI. It did that, but in a limited way. Their display was quite attractive as they had emphasized atlases and folios of paintings that were colorful. However, she realized that their display did pale in comparison to many of the other ones that had artifacts and large display boards, or just larger collections of books and maps. It was probably a mistake to come, but she would never say that to anyone else.

She also realized that it was a bit ironic that, if she hadn't decided to come to the Ottawa event, they wouldn't have discovered the missing books.

Her phone rang and she was a bit surprised to see a Washington area code on the screen.

"Hello, Rhonda Wright here."

"Dr. Wright, this is Agent Efrem Wilson with the FBI. I need to talk to you in confidence about your missing books and some actions that we are taking."

"Well, I'm in Ottawa, Canada right now, at a major history festival."

"Yes, I know. I'm here in Ottawa as well."

"What? Why?"

"That's what I want to talk to you about. Can you meet us for lunch today?"

"I guess so. I have an associate with me who can cover the display."

"Great. Please keep this contact totally confidential."

They all met for lunch at a nearby restaurant. Herb Trawets was introduced to Rhonda Wright as a consulting expert.

"I was certainly surprised to hear from you here," she said. "What's going on?"

"We were hoping to find some leads about your missing books at this gathering of so many bookdealers and collectors, but so far haven't found anything of use. However, we have a new idea that we want to test with you. I'll have Herb explain it."

After Herb had finished his description of what they were suggesting, Rhonda Wright looked at him in total disbelief.

"You want me to agree to have another valuable book stolen?"

"Sort of. We would carefully document the book, take detailed photos, and maybe even add some distinctive marks. Then when it turns up we would hope to backtrack its route."

Wilson added, "And, we will presumably also identify the thief in your organization, but would want to delay apprehending them until the other things play out."

"But what if the book doesn't show up?"

"That's a risk, but we think it's one worth taking. After all, with the attention that the book thefts got when we investigated earlier, I doubt that the thief has been active again. The only reason that the Foxe would be taken in the near term would be the tempting offer that we would be putting into the market. I think that if something does happen we can assume a cause and effect."

"Let me think about it overnight. Besides, I'll need to clear it with the WHI President."

"OK, but we must keep it as confidential as we can. Any slight suspicion will undoubtedly scare the thief off."

As they were departing, Herb asked one more question.

"Director, I have been a bit perplexed about why the Luke Foxe journal is still in your collection when the Thomas James was taken. Have you any idea why the thief might have passed over the Foxe?"

"I don't really know. The James had been in our collection for a long time, maybe 20 years. The Foxe is relatively new for us; it was part of a donated collection that we received less than a year ago. Maybe the thief just hadn't got around to it yet, or was waiting for time to go by and its profile to fade away."

36

The Book Fair had opened to the public at 9:00 a.m. that Friday morning. It was scheduled to go until 2:30 p.m., when it would close for a couple of hours to accommodate the book auction that was going to occur in a nearby auditorium. It would then reopen at 5:00 p.m. and run until 8:00 p.m. It would also be open Saturday from 9:00 a.m. to 6:00 p.m.

The attendance at the opening session was steady, with the typical rush of some keen purchasers at the beginning to search out key books, although the rush always seemed unnecessary as there were one hundred booths to visit and even a cursory first look at all of the books in the front displays and on the back shelves could take a couple of hours. The crowd built steadily through the day, peaking as the time for the auction approached.

A number of dealers noted that the attendees were quite mixed in their approach to their offerings. There were certainly some legitimate collectors who displayed good knowledge of their areas of interest and who were often looking for specific books. However, many more people seemed to be novices, almost sightseeing browsers, attracted by the chance to see rare books related to the Arctic and the adventures of Sir John Franklin that they had been exposed to in the festival displays and at the gala presentation the previous evening.

Thus the dealers spent much more time than usual describing their books and their significance to many of the visitors to their booths. They did this cheerfully and willingly, knowing that a significant new collector could emerge. It had happened before.

At 3:00 that afternoon the book auction took place.

The organization of the auction was a unique combination of commercialism and charity.

As part of the fee dealers paid to be in the book fair, they were required to provide a book for the auction, valued at a minimum of $1,000, although it was made clear that better books were expected. The dealer would receive 80% of the auction price, thus approximating the value they would usually get when selling the books to another dealer, all dependent on the auction price, of course.

BB Bookshelf Auctions, was conducting the event. Normally the auction house would collect a 20% premium on the bid "hammer price."

In this instance they had agreed to 10%, with the other 10% going to charity.

Thus a book that was bid at $1,000 would actually cost the bidder $1,200, with $800 going to the supplying dealer, $100 to the auction house, and $300 to the event's designated charity, The Canadian Historical Education Society.

The 100 books to be auctioned had been on display for the previous few days. A simple catalogue had been prepared with brief descriptions and an expected price range. This value was an educated guess by the auction staff, but based on relatively good awareness of current market values and the prices that the dealers themselves had previously asked. The average total estimate for the auction was essentially one million dollars.

To the surprise of the seasoned dealers, Gunther Shultz, BB Bookshelf's lead auctioneer and major owner from New York, was conducting the auction. He would seldom be present at such a modest event. In reality, he had decided to use the auction as a pretense for a summer vacation in the Ottawa region. The resorts and lakes in the nearby Gatineau Hills were outstanding and he was a keen fisherman. He had arranged for a few of the senior people in BB Bookshelf's Canadian organization to join him for a business strategy workshop. His travel costs and various other expenses would be tax deductible.

Unlike many auctions, the books were not ordered alphabetically by author. Gunther had decided to break them into three groups: pre-1845, the date of Franklin's fateful voyage; 1845 - 1860, the period of the voyage and the subsequent search for Franklin; and post-1860, the time of ongoing exploration of the Arctic and determination to reach the North Pole.

There were about twenty-five books in the first section.

The early Middleton and Dobbs books of the 1740s that debated the possibility of a Northwest Passage out of Hudson's Bay got the auction off to a good start when they jointly attracted $40,000.

Barrington's *Miscellanies* of 1781 that implored the British to search for the North Pole achieved $5,000, more than predicted.

The significant Parry, Ross and Scoresby voyages of the 1820s also got good prices.

If there was any early trend, it was that the more valuable books got full value bids, but that the lower-end books were overbid by quite a bit. For example, Barrow's 1846 book that summarized all of the *Arctic Voyages of Discovery* from 1818 – 1845 sold for $4,000, twice its estimate.

It seemed like some of the people in the audience were determined to get a souvenir of the event and thus competed aggressively for the less expensive books. The relatively common books about John Franklin's early overland trips to the Arctic in the 1820s were seriously overbid at $6,000.

The core of the auction were the fifty or so books related to the search for Franklin's lost expedition, and the same trend continued.

Key collectibles such as the voyages of Goodsir, Inglefield and Kennedy sold well. Key events captured in books like Rae's first determination of what happened to John Franklin and McClintock's final confirmation got good premiums.

The story of McClure's disastrous voyage, but claim to first discovery of a Northwest Passage, even though he walked for much of it over the frozen ocean, sold for a premium $10,000.

The post-Franklin books were generally more common, but attracted good prices from the souvenir hunters.

In the end, everyone was very satisfied with a total auction value of $1.2 million.

The book fair reopened from 5:00 – 8:00. Dealers were happy to see more activity than in the earlier session. The auction seemed to have motivated people to buy.

37

The next morning, the group met again for breakfast. Wilson, Watkins and Trawets were all anxious to hear what Rhonda Wright was going to say. After settling into a booth and ordering, they looked at her expectantly.

"I have thought a great deal about your proposal and have talked with the President of WHI. It has not been easy to decide. Our first responsibility is to WHI. To put even one book at risk is difficult, because it could impact our reputation with employees, public supporters, donors, everyone.

"However, we do recognize that we have already lost some books, and don't really know the scope of that. Thus, if it all becomes public that we have had a large problem, we will suffer the reputational hit anyway. And we know secrets don't last long in today's public dialogues. So, our best action is to be proactive in solving the problem. We can probably go along with your proposal, but have many questions."

"OK," said Wilson. "Ask away."

"Can we put in cameras or some kind of surveillance to watch the book and see what happens?"

"We considered that but the answer has to be 'no.' There's no way to install cameras or other monitoring hardware without people inside knowing. You are a small group in a relatively small space and we don't know who to trust. Anyone from your curators to the security staff could notice and then everyone would know. They would inevitably share the information as just part of noticing increased security."

"Can we put some tracer on the book?"

"Again, that's too risky. We're dealing with a sophisticated group of thieves and probably money launderers. They would very likely check for that, given everything that has transpired so far. They will be very cautious."

"Then how will you confirm any book that surfaces is ours?"

"Herb suggests that we can take detailed photos to highlight even minor blemishes or tears, which will be like fingerprints. We could even put some minor marks of our own that would not be noticed as unusual."

"If we aren't monitoring things closely, how will we know who steals the book if it does happen. It will all be after the fact."

"We could put cameras on the outside of the building and then maybe correlate comings and goings with the book disappearing."

"Maybe. If the book does disappear after hours or in slow times. What if Security detects the book being taken out? We believe that everyone is more vigilant now."

"That's possible. But, the thief knows all of that and so, if the book is taken, they will probably have some kind of plan. Worst case, we have the thief and try to work forward to find the network. That will likely be more difficult than working backwards from the book surfacing with us,"

After a pause, Rhoda Wright said, "OK. How do we proceed?"

Herb spoke up. "Today at the book fair I will carefully spread the word that I am looking for some specific books for a special client. Even though I'm retired, other dealers would not be surprised that I do some scouting."

Wilson smiled. Wright wouldn't know of Herb's reputation as being the main rare-book supplier to the President of the United States.

"Some books?" asked Wright.

"Yes, one book would look a bit strange. I'll name a couple of books. They won't necessarily be at WHI but will be large books or volumes, such that they are not likely to be stolen by our thief."

"Do you actually think the book thief is here in Ottawa?"

"Probably not, actually. But the rare-book world is a bit of a closed shop. Word should get around. If not, we won't have lost anything, not even your book."

"What if someone actually brings you the requested books, but not ours?"

"Then I will make a deal to buy them or not. I am a book dealer you know."

"How will we scan and mark the book?"

"I'm sure we have some time. Spreading my message and then time for people to react will not happen quickly. I can come down to WHI next week. Some evening, or even on a Sunday, when you're sure no one will be around to take notice, you can take me in to the WHI and I'll photograph and carefully mark the book. Just be sure no one else is in the area."

They agreed to the plan.

Wilson's final thought was that, if this worked, he would pursue it aggressively since it would mean that there was a large operation in play. If not, it would be time to tell the Director that it was time to shut the pursuit down. More resources for this long-shot play would not be justified.

38

Shortly after 9:00 a.m. Herb returned to the book fair. Over the next few hours he wandered through the area, talking to all of the dealers.

With the larger dealers, who he knew quite well, those conversations were very relaxed and conversational. They would chat about the fair in general, the previous day's auction and the festival events. At some point Herb would mention to them that he was on the lookout for a few specific books for a client. Inevitably they would kid him about being retired and he would say that book scouting was just like retirement, travelling but with a purpose. Most of them would also presume that he was acting for President Cartwright without ever asking.

He had decided that he would mention four books, all related to the Arctic, relatively rare and valuable. Of course he mentioned the Foxe and for good measure added the James, since they were usually linked with each other. He emphasized that his client would pay a good premium for them. He also added the Sarychev text and atlas of 1802 related to the early exploration of the Bering Strait and the Pacific entrance to the Arctic, plus the Creswell folio of sketches from the McClure expedition that was credited with the first discovery of a Northwest Passage. He doubted that either of those would be part of any theft scam since they were very large in size.

His conversation with Simon Katz was typical.

"Hello, Simon."

"Hi, Herb. Still slumming?"

"Oh, it has been a nice few days. I enjoyed the area and the festival activities. I thought the presentation on Franklin was well done. Our conversations last evening were insightful."

"I agree with that."

"How has the fair and the auction gone?"

"OK. There were a few serious collectors here. Also some curiosity seekers, I guess I would call them, who did buy a few things."

"It has been good to see everyone. I'll be heading out later this afternoon. I wanted to mention to you that I am on the lookout for a few books, none of which I found here."

"Oh," said Simon with a bit of a smile, "What are those?"

"Well, a Foxe and a James that I can pay a good premium for, as well as a Sarychev and a Creswell."

"Sure, those are tough to find. I probably have three clients looking for a Foxe."

"Well, if you find one, don't forget me. I can be competitive."

"Right. Good luck."

"Take care, Simon. I'll see you around."

"Safe travels, Herb."

His approach to the dealers he didn't know was a little more formal. He would introduce himself, even if he had chatted with them in his first round of the booths on set-up day. He would explain he was on the lookout for some specific books that he hadn't found at the fair and asked the dealers to contact him if they came across them. He would leave them a business card with the four books written on the back.

His conversation with Alexander Rusti of Philadelphia was typical.

"Hi, I'm Herb Trawets, a retired book dealer. You might remember that I was wandering through your booth the other day."

"Hi. I'm Alexander Rusti, but everyone calls me Sasha. I think I recall seeing you. How can I help you?"

"I've been looking for a few specific books but had no luck here at the fair. I thought I would mention that to various dealers so if you come across them you might contact me. I have a client who will pay a good premium for them.'

"Sure, what are they?"

"There are two early exploration voyages into Hudson's Bay by Thomas James and Luke Foxe. Their journals are of high interest. There is the folio of Arctic illustrations by Creswell from the McClure expedition. Also, the Sarychev atlas and text from the Billings expedition."

"Wow, those are big ticket items. I don't usually see things like that but I will keep a lookout."

"Thanks. Here is my card; I have written the names of the books on the back."

"OK."

"Good to meet you, Sasha. Take care."

"You too."

After Herb left, Sasha contemplated what he had heard. It seemed that the James journal was turning up in his world a lot. He even had the one that he had recently purchased from the New England dealer. For some reason that he couldn't quite figure out, he had held that information back. He wanted to be careful. He decided he would try to check out Mr. Herb Trawets first. Also, he had to research where he might find a Foxe. There could be big money involved here if he could get a set of the two books.

39

Back in Philadelphia, Sasha Rusti took stock of what he has heard in Ottawa. The premise was simple. There was a big payout for supplying Herb Trawets with a James and a Foxe. That could be $400,000 or more.

He had a James. He didn't think it was the same one as the one they stole from the WHI years ago, but he would check it over thoroughly again. He had seen the first one but that was a long time ago. Back then all he had looked for were any obvious marks or stamps that would link it to the WHI or any previous owner who had donated it to them. He had cleaned out one bookplate.

He needed a Foxe. He was very surprised when he started looking around that he found one in the first place he looked: the WHI collection! Could they possibly go back there again?

Who was Herb Trawets? A search of American bookdealers easily identified him as the former owner of Herb's Books in Seattle, now retired to California. His real name was Yrrab Trawets. He had been fairly involved in bookdealers' associations over the years and appeared to be well-respected. That was about it.

That Friday Sasha went down to his local pub, as was quite usual. He watched Hugo make his normal rounds of the tables, gathering the wagers. After that, Hugo sat beside him and ordered a beer, as had been happening for years now.

"Hi, Sasha. I missed you last week. How was Ottawa?"

"Fine. It's a nice place and I sold some books."

"Good."

"I also picked up a lead that could be a real opportunity for us, but I'm not sure about it."

"What is it?"

"Not here. I think you should contact Tony and we should all meet, say Monday at the book store?"

Hugo looked at him with a raised eyebrow.

"Are we going back into business?"

"Maybe."

Monday morning Hugo and Tony walked into Sasha's Metro Rare Books. They settled into chairs with big mugs of coffee in hand.

Tony started, "So?" He always got right to the point.

Sasha described what had happened in Ottawa and what he had done over the past week.

"You have a James you think is clean. You think this guy Trawets is straight. We need to steal the Foxe from WHI. Then we make a lot of money. Is that it?"

"Right. If we think we can get the Foxe."

"We shut down all of the book activities with the five pickers months ago, when the FBI was nosing around again and the alert notices went out. Why is it safe to start again?"

Sasha smiled at Tony referring to the book thieves as pickers, just as if the books were fruit or vegetables. "I don't know for sure, but there have been no other investigations or follow-ups that we know about. I guess the best way to test that is to ask your pickers."

"Surely the security at the institutions has been increased."

"Again, ask the guys."

"How many Foxes are out there? Can you get another one?"

"Very rare. Maybe turn up in an auction of a collection once a decade. I didn't find one in any of the other institutions we have been getting books from."

"You know, there is always a time to walk away. We have done very well. There is the old saying that pigs get fed and hogs get slaughtered. We have been good pigs, taking most of the money in the chain of book sales. Why take the risk for more?"

Sasha was a bit taken aback. He had been a bit nervous about the idea but had expected Tony to jump at it when he finally proposed it.

"Tony, what's the real risk? Let's just do the one book; keep the other four operations shut down for now. As you have said before, the pickers are isolated from many contacts."

Hugo spoke up. "Sasha, in our business it's all about risk management, or should I say risk aversion. Our goal isn't to have a low profile, it's to have no profile. Of course, that's not really doable but we always think that way. If we get a problem it could trigger consequences on all the money we have moved and made over the years. The Feds have been snooping around for more than a year now and so the risk is higher. I agree there has been no activity lately, but?"

"I understand. OK. But is there really much risk in trying for one more book that could make us hundreds of thousands of dollars?"

After a long pause, Tony said, "We'll find out what the picker says."

40

Herb Trawets flew out of Ottawa, not heading back home to California but to Philadelphia, so that he could meet with Rhonda Wright in the coming week to set up the Luke Foxe journal.

Wright didn't return until Tuesday, having stayed with the display in Ottawa and overseeing the organization of the packing up and shipment of all the materials on Monday.

Len Nelson, the more technical agent on Wilson's team, also came to Philadelphia, having been briefed by Wilson and Watkins.

The three of them met for dinner at a restaurant far away from the WHI on Tuesday evening. It was a caution. Herb didn't want to be seen by the staff at the WHI since he wasn't sure who might have been in Ottawa.

"Well, how do we proceed?" asked Rhonda Wright.

"The concept is quite simple," said Herb. "You will take me to the WHI at some quiet off-hours time and arrange for me to be with the Foxe book for a while in a private place. I will take detailed photos of the book and look for a way to place some extra identifying marks on it. Then you return the book to the shelves and we wait to see what happens."

Len Nelson spoke up. "I should also be present. My presence will verify that this is a formal investigation procedure. I have brought a high resolution camera that we can use."

Wright responded after some thought. "We can probably do that. Most staff members generally leave the WHI right after we close at 5:00 p.m. It would not be unusual for me to stay late, especially since I have been away for the past week. I can check to be sure the place is quiet and then call you to come over, say about 6:00. I can leave a message with security that I'm expecting you to discuss some donations. That's also not terribly unusual at that hour since people do often have daytime commitments. Identify yourself at the entrance by name; don't add on your employers or connections. No questions will be asked."

"How soon can we do that?"

"Let's do it tomorrow evening. If something doesn't feel right, I'll call you and cancel it and we can try again the next day."

That's how it all worked out.

Herb and Len arrived just after 6:00 p.m. and after some simple check-in procedures were escorted to Rhonda Wright's office.

She had determined that the Institute was very quiet that evening and called them to come. In the time between the call and their arrival she had wandered through the Rare Books Gallery, looking over the materials that had arrived that day from Ottawa, and casually picked the Foxe book from the shelves and took it to her office. There was nothing in the internal monitoring system to notice that.

Once in her office, Len Nelson set up his camera on a small tripod and, working with Herb, laid open the book. They took photos of every page of the book. It wasn't that large.

In the midst of all that, Herb said, "This will be as good as fingerprints. The book is almost four hundred years old. Every page has marks, stains, tears and folds. If we get this book back from someone else it will be easy to confirm it."

"Didn't you also suggest that we place some unique markings that would make the identification even more absolute?" asked Rhonda.

"Yes, but it must be very subtle."

"Any ideas, now that you have the book?"

"Old books invariably have pencil markings on them, usually placed by owners or dealers as part of their inventory management. Any such obvious marks would undoubtedly be removed by any competent thief to destroy any unwanted provenance. But I'm thinking that a couple of simple pencil marks, placed in the folds of the pages would not likely be noticed or remarked upon. I think I will place a minor mark in the folds of pages 16 and 35, reflecting the year of publication, 1635."

"Good. So, I will see you out and then, when returning to shut down my activities for the evening, I'll return the book to its place in the collections."

"OK. How will you monitor for the book's disappearance?" asked Len.

"I have many reasons to wander into the collections area. I know where the book belongs. I should be able to detect its absence without getting too close."

"Fine. Just don't get to hovering too often so as to attract attention."

With that, they dispersed.

41

Alberto contacted Dennis at home. "We need to talk."

"What? You're kidding."

"No, let's just talk about things. I'll meet you at the park bench on Saturday afternoon."

After they hung up, Dennis sat back and took stock. He had been involved with Alberto for many years and had stolen a lot of books. They had shut down operations some time ago as a result of the FBI investigations. He had managed to avoid detection, or even suspicion, as far as he could tell. Why would he get started again?

Of course, there was the money. He had made maybe $300,000 over the ten-plus years. It wasn't a huge amount, given the time span, but it had made his life better.

He also thought about his experience at the Ottawa festival. It had been a nice break and he had enjoyed the time exploring the city's attractions. Staffing the display at the festival was fine, although he found it somewhat boring as he would answer the same questions over and over for the people who came by. He wondered if Rhonda Wright thought it had been worthwhile for the WHI; he didn't think so.

He had been fascinated and a bit bothered by his visit to the antiquarian book fair that was part of the festival. In spite of his involvement with rare books for a long time, he had never actually been to a commercial book fair before. He knew that the Ottawa fair was a relatively small one, but he was still amazed by the proliferation of valuable books. The range and quality of the books was high. Some of the larger dealers had more than 100 books with a total value of well over a million dollars.

It had left him feeling depressed. He, with his high education and prestigious job in the institutional world, made a relatively modest living while those shopkeepers made huge amounts. Somehow this irrationally made him feel less guilty about having stolen the books. However, he knew no one else would see it that way.

What would Alberto want? There was always an undertone of risk and threat when he dealt with him.

On Saturday they met in the park.

"How was your trip?" Alberto asked.

"Fine. What do you want to talk about?" Dennis replied, more curtly than he intended, but he was anxious.

"How have things been going at WHI? Have there been any more searches? Has the FBI turned up again? Do you feel any suspicion has arisen?"

Dennis stared at Alberto for a minute after that barrage of questions. Where was he going?

"Things have been quiet; normal is the best description I guess. The fact that the Director took me on the Ottawa trip seems to show there is no suspicion. Why?"

"We would like you to get another book for us. Can you do that?"

Again, a pause. "Security and general alertness has certainly picked up. I don't know if I could do it again. Why start again now, so soon?"

"Apparently there is a new opportunity for us with a specific book. That's why we need to know if you can get it."

"What's the book?"

"Apparently it's a lot like the first book you took years ago. It's another Arctic journal, this time by Luke Foxe in the 1600s."

"Oh, not another Arctic book! That's the one area that has drawn all of the attention. That makes me more concerned."

"Of course. Concerned and cautious. But, can you do it?"

Dennis was lost in thought for a while. "I don't know. I'll need to think about it for a while. I would need some new maneuver. I'll need to look at our current layout with a different perspective, the security protocols in particular. Give me some time."

"Let's meet again next week. You can tell me what you have decided. We have done a lot over the years; you always come through."

Was that a threat? Dennis wasn't sure.

"OK, next week. But, if I find a way to do this I will need a much larger payment. It's going to be much more difficult and risky."

Alberto just smiled, but did nod his head slightly.

A week later, they met again. Dennis got right to the point.

"I may have an idea. However, it will take some time to set up as it will involve a number of steps. Also, I might have to abandon it if things get suspicious along the way."

"That's good. I am very pleased that you will try."

"About the payment. I will need much more than in the past. I did some research. A Luke Foxe sold at an auction of the Cushing Collection some years ago for $150,000. It has to be worth more now, maybe $200,000. I think I should get twenty-five percent, $50,000, if I get the book."

"Wow, Dennis. That's a lot of money. You certainly must appreciate that when we dispose of these rare books we must take a heavy discount. Many others get involved before it finally reaches a collector. That amount is too much."

"Maybe normally, Alberto. However, last week you said that you had a specific opportunity for this book. I think you will be getting a big payout and I need some of that for the risk I am taking."

"We understand that but you need to be reasonable. Let's say we pay ten times the usual payment, $30,000? That's very generous."

Dennis realized that Alberto had come to the meeting with that prepared reply. Was he just negotiating or was he 'making an offer that he couldn't refuse.' Emboldened by the frustration that had been building since Ottawa, he said, "If I can see all of this through I must get more. Let's split the difference and call it $40,000."

Alberto smiled. In his world he didn't get many counter-offers when he said something was very generous. However, Tony Esposito had instructed him that he could agree to such a payment. They knew Dennis was taking a big risk and they might never even get the book.

"Agreed," he said.

42

Dennis worked out his plan for extracting the Luke Foxe book from the WHI in great detail.

First, he needed to create a cover story. He decided that he would write an extended paper for publication in one of the book industry journals, Books History. Inspired by the Ottawa Arctic festival, and the need to gain access to the Foxe, he titled his paper 'Frobisher to Franklin – How the World Learned about the Arctic.' He made sure everyone in the Rare Books section of WHI knew about his latest project.

After a few days of making notes from various books he collected from the stacks, carefully returning them at the end of each day, he gathered up a few books to take home for weekend research. He filled out the triplicate forms and packed them in his book briefcase, of course with no extra book in the lower compartment. The Foxe was not part of his selection.

As he left the WHI, the security guard checked his paperwork and briefcase, asking him to take each book out for a cross-check. Yes, security had been tightened. No, he wouldn't be taking the Foxe out in the old way of simply hiding it in the bottom of his briefcase.

On many afternoons in the time he could set aside for individual projects, he continued the research for his paper. He quite got into it and knew he would end up with a publishable result. This belief, and his attendant quiet enthusiasm, totally convinced his co-workers that he was committed to it.

Then one day he included the Foxe journal in the group of books he gathered, returning it at the end of the session. A few days later he did the same thing but he purposely returned the book to the wrong place on the shelves. The printing on the spine of the book said Luke Foxe Journal. He had also gathered a book by Lyon about the Parry journey in the 1820s. He returned them beside each other, something that could be explained as just a minor error. Filing the book in the L-initial section was just a slipup on reading Luke rather than Foxe as the key name.

No one seemed to notice.

A few days later he again gathered the Foxe journal with his selections but this time he returned it to its right place.

The next phase of his plan was to identify a few valuable books that were in poor shape, having damaged covers, stained title pages or torn maps. The Foxe was somewhat tattered. There was a budget for book restorations that could be accessed by the curators in collaboration with the in-house restorer, Emma Johnston.

He approached Emma.

"Hey, Emma, I have a project for you. I've been using many of our Arctic books for my research on the paper I'm writing. I've noticed that a few of the special books are in relatively poor shape and think they are worth getting restored. I saw similar books at the Ottawa event and the books are certainly more impressive when they are fixed up. Here are the books; what do you think?"

He handed her four books. The Foxe was not one of them.

"Well, Dennis, I agree these could be made much better. The scope is beyond what I can do here but we could send them out to a specialist. We have funds in the budget but haven't been doing it much because of the general attitude of tightening down these days."

"I'm glad you agree. What do we do next?"

"It requires a requisition, describing what needs to be done and providing the justification, which Katherine will need to sign. I am quite tied up in a project right now but I could probably get to it in a week or so."

"I would be happy to do that paperwork, since it was my idea that started it," Dennis said, holding his breath. He had known that Emma was very busy with a project for an upcoming display and had timed his approach accordingly. He hoped for this opportunity.

"OK. Sure. Thanks,"

"Who do you usually use for that type of work?"

"Cooper Best is excellent and reasonable. He will ensure that any restorations are totally in keeping with the time of the publication. It's amazing how many books get restored in fancy bindings that are quite inappropriate; being typical of periods centuries apart sometimes"

Over the next couple of days, Dennis wrote up the descriptions of the four books with an explanation of the restoration work required and how the inherent value of the books justified it. He took the bundle of paper to Katherine Clay's office.

"Hi, Katherine. Got a minute?"

"Hi, Dennis. Sure, come on in. What's on your mind?"

"As you know I'm working on an Arctic history project and have been utilizing many of our relevant books for reference. I have identified a few books that are very valuable but in poor shape that I think should be restored. I've talked this over with Emma and she agrees. I have a proposal here for you to look at."

With that, Dennis handed the bundle of paper to Katherine, who took a few minutes to glance through it.

"David, this all seems to be in order and I can see why you have proposed this, but I am not sure it's warranted. You know funds are getting tighter."

David had anticipated this response and had prepared a reply, even if some of it was a bit of a fabrication.

"Katherine, I understand. Emma and I considered that before we agreed to bring the proposal to you. Emma said that she had been avoiding using the budget for that reason. However, she is also concerned that, if we don't spend some funds in this area, the category might just be eliminated in future budgets. We do need to maintain the quality of our collections over the long term."

Katherine was sympathetic to the plea; after all WHI and its collections were her life's work.

"How much will this cost?"

"I spoke to Cooper Best and described what was required. He said he could do all of the work for $8,000. Emma says he is the best around for this type of work and is reasonable with his charges. It certainly seems worthwhile to me."

After a pause, "Alright, I agree. It's not a lot of money and we do need to protect our books and our budgets."

With that, Katherine signed the requisition document and the various attachments, such as the triplicate book-removal forms.

The final stage was the trickiest. This was where everything could unravel. Dennis didn't know how he could talk his way out of it if he was caught. A simple story that he had intended to include the Foxe in the paperwork probably wouldn't work.

It was Friday afternoon. He rounded up a cardboard box, some packing foam popcorn and some heavy brown wrapping paper. He placed the five books in the carton, sealed it and addressed it: Cooper Best, Best Bindings, Box 542, 123 Red Rock Road, Radnor, PA.

Then he went over to the general administration desk and approached Chelsea Birmingham, the junior staff person.

"Hey, Chelsea. I have a package that needs to be couriered out. Here is all of the paperwork, signed off by Katherine. Would you organize that, please?"

"OK, Dennis. I guess I can do that. You should have had us wrap all that for you; that's what we do. You didn't need to have done all that."

"No, problem. I know everyone is busy."

"I should have actually checked the contents against the triplicate forms."

"I guess, but I did that. The one copy is in there with the books for when they return. The other two copies are there on top for your files."

"OK. I'll send it out."

"Thanks, Chelsea."

Dennis had counted on his established seniority and Chelsea's relative inexperience to carry the day. It had worked.

After work, Dennis drove to Radnor, about one hour away. He had rented a mail delivery box in a general shop in a normal strip mall. It had been easy to give it the name Best Bindings on the paperwork. The clerk didn't care and the name sounded very generic.

He walked into the shop and went to his box. Inside was a note, saying Large Parcel at Desk. The clerk quickly located the box and gave it to Dennis. There was no fuss.

Returning to his car, Dennis quickly opened the box and removed the books. He placed the four books destined for restoration in another box that he had prepared with Best Bindings correct address on it. It was nearby, also in Radnor.

Then he went down the street to a UPS courier shop and paid for it to be sent onwards overnight. He would phone Cooper Best in the morning to confirm he had received the package.

Arriving home, he finally let out a deep breath. Then, with a smile on his face he called Alberto.

"I have it."

43

Rhonda Wright had been distressed and distracted ever since the evening when FBI Agent Nelson and Herb Trawets had come to the WHI and photographed and marked the Luke Foxe journal.

She kept second-guessing her decision to go along with the sting operation. She couldn't decide if she actually wanted the book to disappear or not. How could they just simply let a valuable book be stolen? How good it would be to catch whoever had stolen the other books from the WHI. Back and forth.

At first, she would wander into the Rare Books area each day on some pretext and casually glance at the location on the shelves where she knew the Foxe resided. However, after quite a few days nothing had happened and she was concerned that her constant presence might seem suspicious. After all, if the book did disappear, all she was going to do was call the FBI and hopefully wait for it to surface again. They weren't going to acknowledge to anyone that the book was gone. She reduced the frequency of her visits.

Then, one day a few weeks after it all started, she walked by the bookshelf and the Foxe was not there. She almost stumbled as she reacted but no one was in the immediate area to notice.

She returned to her office as casually as she could muster, closed the door, and called Agent Wilson at the FBI.

"The book is gone," she blurted out as soon as he answered. She realized that she was a bit flustered.

"Take it easy," responded Wilson. "This is what we hoped for. Now we just need to wait for it to resurface. I will inform Herb Trawets to be prepared for an approach. This could take some time; be patient."

"Yes, I know."

"And, be sure you do not do anything to raise an alarm. If the thieves know we are aware it's missing, they could bail out on our scheme out of extreme caution. The book could disappear for a long time and maybe end up somewhere else."

"Yes, again I know. We talked about all of that. I will sit tight."

Then, a few days later, Rhonda walked through the Rare Books area again, for a totally different purpose, and the Foxe was back on the shelf.

She gasped, thankfully at a low level. She had to restrain herself from actually going over to it and checking it out. That could be a big mistake.

Back in her office, she again called Wilson.

"The book is back on the shelf."

"What? How could that have happened?"

"I don't know."

"Are you sure it's the right book?"

"No, I didn't dare go and touch it. That seemed too risky."

"Right; of course. Can you check it out later when no one else is around?"

"I guess so. I could stay late and when I'm sure the area is cleared out I could check the book. It will only take a moment."

"OK. Do that and call me again later."

A few hours later she was back on the phone with Wilson.

"It's the same book alright. It even has the small marks that Herb Trawets put in it."

"Have you any idea where the book could have been for a few days?'

"No, not really. Books do get misfiled but that seems strange, especially for it to turn up in the right place again."

"Maybe the thief was setting things up to see if anything would happen?"

"Do you think so? That's disturbing, since it would mean that there really is a thief in our midst."

"In any case, I don't think you've done anything to alarm anyone. I guess we just go back to waiting again."

A month later, on a Monday afternoon, Rhonda Wright was in the area again and the Foxe was gone again.

A call to Wilson quickly followed.

"It's gone."

"Are you sure?"

"It's not on the shelf and there was no other activity in the gallery."

"Well, maybe this is it. We are back to waiting. But, do check back from time to time to make sure it doesn't reappear like last time."

The Foxe did not appear again.

44

Sasha Rusti held the Luke Foxe book in his hands. Hugo Cici had just delivered it. He had been thinking of this possibility for many weeks.

"Well, Hugo, there it is. Now we must plan our path forward very carefully.

"First, I'll examine it very carefully to be sure there are no WHI identifying marks or stamps anywhere. Then, I will probably modify the book a bit, maybe trim some edges and spruce up the binding. The book is so rare that minor changes won't make any difference in its value and they'll help conceal its history. Finally, I will get a couple of decorated leather boxes made for it and the James that I have. That should enhance the appeal and thus the value of the pair as a set.

"We'll need to establish a chain of ownership buys and sells through our network so that if necessary we can buck things back to the bottom. Once we've done that, let's totally shut down the first entity in the chain and disperse its assets and lose its records. Again, if there is a problem we need a dead end somewhere.

"When we're ready I will contact Herb Trawets. That's a bit of a change for us. I haven't been the seller of record for many of our previous books, just a few particular ones in earlier times where I could use my contacts to get a better price. More recently they've all gone to other dealers or customers through one of our intermediate entities. However, we can't just sell these books on to a major dealer or online to an unknown customer; we would lose too much value.

"Notionally, these two books are worth $300,000 or more. We would maybe clear $250,000 to a big dealer. However, Trawets has indicated a true premium is available. We have to deal directly with him; we could possibly double our take that way. That's why we took the chance to get the Foxe."

Hugo nodded.

45

Herb Trawets was in his California home office when the phone rang. It was midmorning on a Monday.

"Hello, Herb Trawets here."

"Mr. Trawets, this is Alexander Rusti calling. You may recall we met at the book fair in Ottawa a couple of months ago."

"Oh, yes," Herb said, a bit hesitantly. He had a vague recollection of meeting Rusti. After all, he had talked to about one hundred dealers. "How can I help you?"

"You mentioned to me at the time that you were looking for copies of the Arctic exploration journals by Thomas James and Luke Foxe. Are you still looking?"

Herb took a deep breath. Could this really be happening?

"Yes I am, Alexander. Do you have copies?"

"Call me Sasha, by the way; everyone does. Yes, I have been able to locate copies of both documents."

"Can you describe them for me?"

"They are both complete and in very good condition. They are bound with matching boards and spines in the style of the period. They are both enclosed in well-made storage boxes, again embossed in a style to match the books."

Herb's first thought was it might not be the Foxe from the WHI, but who knows? Modifications might have been made.

"Where are they?"

"I have them at my shop in Philadelphia."

"Well, I am certainly very interested. I will need to be in touch with my customer to get his confirmation but that should happen quickly. Can you email me some photos of the books so that I can give him a sense of them, say of the bindings and the title pages?"

"Sure, that's easy to do."

"What shall I tell him your asking price is?"

"Actually, I would like you to make an offer. As you know, the books are quite rare and there will be others who would be very interested in them. I may need to create a simple auction."

Herb smiled. Sasha was going to get the maximum bid, which was smart of him.

"OK, I'll get back to you as soon as I talk to my customer. I just ask that you not dispose of the books until we can make you an offer. I am sure we will be competitive."

"Fine. I'll send you some photos and wait for you to get back to me."

After they hung up, Sasha sat and reran the conversation through his mind. Everything seemed normal; Trawets had responded as he would have expected.

He had photos of the books at the ready; that was an obvious ask by Trawets. He downloaded them into an email and sent them onwards. He assumed he would hear back relatively quickly. His suggestion that there could be other buyers should keep things moving along.

Herb also reviewed the call. There was nothing specific to tie this approach to the WHI book other than the timing.

As he was preparing to call Wilson, his email flashed and the photos from Rusti arrived. "That was quick," he thought, but he wasn't too surprised. Rusti had obviously prepared well for his call, quite a normal thing to do for items that were so valuable.

Herb opened his file of the photos they had taken of the Foxe journal at the WHI and compared them to the new photos. The bindings were quite different and the pages of the new book had a tighter trim, but that could be easily done to change a book's appearance. The title page was cleaner, again a normal upgrading process. There were two small spots in the lower right corner that seemed to match the WHI copy. They were fainter but definitely there. That wasn't conclusive, but certainly encouraging. Once he could examine the whole book he would be able to decide for sure.

He called Wilson. It was early afternoon in Washington.

"Agent Wilson, Herb Trawets calling from California. I have received a call about a Luke Foxe journal."

"Great, that's great. I was starting to get concerned that our plan wasn't going to work."

"Well, don't get too far ahead of this yet. We don't know if it's our book for sure."

"Tell me what happened."

Herb described the call he had with Sasha Rusti and the photos he had examined.

"So, don't those spots confirm it's the same book?"

"Strong possibility is what I would say. You probably don't conclude fingerprints are a match with only a couple of minor similarities."

"OK, OK. So, what's the next step?"

"As we have discussed, we need to get our hands on the book. I will call Rusti back and confirm our keen interest.

"Often, in the bookselling world, a dealer will send books to another dealer on consignment, for inspection. I don't know if he would do that here or not. He did imply there may be others interested. I will tell him that I can go to Philadelphia to see the books. For something so valuable that would not be unusual. Of course our only real agenda is to see the book and confirm if it's the WHI copy. If it's not, we will just back away. We are not going to get into a bidding war for a legitimate other copy."

"Right. Let me know what happens with the next call. When you do meet I can be nearby to take action if you confirm it's our book."

"Sure, but remember that even if it is the WHI copy Rusti may not know that it was stolen."

Herb called Sasha.

After a quick greeting Herb said, "Sasha, my client is definitely interested. He's located back east, not far from you. We agreed that I should fly back there and meet with you. I can examine the books in detail and then give him a report. We could proceed from there."

"That sounds fine. How soon can you come?" Sasha wanted to keep the process going.

"I can fly from LAX tomorrow morning and be in Philadelphia tomorrow evening, given the distances and time zone changes. I could meet you on Wednesday morning, if that works for you."

"Certainly. I'll see you then. Given the time changes, do you want to come at 10:00 a.m.? Not too early I hope."

"Sounds fine."

"Herb, have you determined a price you will pay yet?" again pressing a bit. Sasha hoped it sounded like he was being a bit naïve, being a smaller-time dealer interacting with a bigger player.

Herb smiled, picking up on that obvious ploy.

"Of course, as always it will all depend on the condition of the books. All I can say now is that we would likely be in the $400,000 range."

"Thanks, see you on Wednesday." Sasha smiled. With that as the opening number, he knew they were going to strike it big.

46

Herb arrived at Metro Rare Books as scheduled.

Sasha greeted him at the door; he had obviously been waiting for Herb's arrival. Herb noticed that the sign in the window said "Closed."

They walked back to a small but comfortable seating area where Sasha had coffee waiting.

"Welcome, again," said Sasha as they sat down.

"This is a very nice shop you have," observed Herb.

"Yes, I've been here for a few decades now. It's comforting to be surrounded by the familiar layout and all of the memories. But in reality I should close up. The walk-in business is getting smaller every year. I do most of my business online from my computer now. Even my catalogues go out electronically and most orders come back the same way."

"I understand completely. When I finally closed my bookstore in Seattle I had the same dilemma, but I was ready to retire."

"I'm getting close to that point, I think."

With that initial conversation, they both relaxed a bit, but they both also knew the next few minutes were going to be important, although for different reasons.

"Well, Sasha, can I see the books?"

"Certainly; you didn't come all this way for coffee and chitchat."

Sasha took Herb over to a counter in the corner of the store. Laid out were two small, embossed-leather boxes with simple labels engraved on the spines, James and Foxe.

Herb, not wanting to look too anxious, opened them, exposing the two journals. They had certainly been rebound, and the Foxe looked nothing like the book he had seen at the WHI.

He said, "They certainly are impressive on first glance. Where did you get them?"

Sasha replied easily, "I obtained the James some time ago from a dealer in New England. The Foxe I found recently from an internet scan of rare book sites, a technique that I routinely employ. Once I had them both, I cleaned them up and had them bound and boxed in matching styles. Then I called you."

Herb nodded. That seemed credible.

He first opened the James and found it to be in good condition. He had no real data to compare it to the James that had disappeared from the WHI.

Then he opened the Foxe. It was certainly cleaner and neater than the version that he had seen at the WHI. The two spots on the title page were discernable, but very faint. He knew he would want to compare photos of every page when he got the chance.

He casually opened the book to page 16 and slightly bent the book back. There was a small pencil mark inside the fold. With his heart pounding and holding his breath, he did the same thing at page 35. Same thing!

"Sasha, these books are amazing. My client will be ecstatic. Give me a moment, I want to call him."

"Sure. Take your time. I'll wait for you at the front of the store."

Herb called Wilson. "It's here," he said.

"I'll be there in minutes."

Herb returned to the books and looked at them with a sense of admiration. They were special.

Sasha came back.

"Are we good?"

"My client will be here in a few minutes. He wants to see them himself, now that I have seen them."

Sasha frowned a bit, wondering why the client didn't come with Herb in the first place.

A short time later there was a knock at the front door of the bookstore. Sasha went to the front and opened the door."

"Good morning, Sir. I am Agent Wilson with the FBI; these other people with me are also FBI agents. We would ask you to step aside and let us in. We have a warrant and reason to believe that there are stolen goods on the property."

NORTH-VVEST FOX:
OR,
Fox from the North-weſt paſſage.

BEGINNING

VVith King ARTHVR, MALGA, OCTHVR,
the two ZENIS of _Iſland_, _Eſtotiland_, and _Dorgia_;
Following with briefe Abſtracts of the Voyages of _Cabot_,
Frobiſher, _Davis_, _Weymouth_, _Knight_, _Hudſon_, _Button_, _Gib-
bons_, _Bylot_, _Baffin_, _Hawbridge_. Together with the
Courſes, Diſtance, Latitudes, Longitudes, Variations,
Depths of Seas, Sets of Tydes, Currents, Races,

Mr. IAMES HALL; three Voyages to _Groyland_, with a
Topographicall deſcription of the Countrie, the Saluages
liſes and Treacheries, how our Men haue beene ſlayne
by them there, with the Commodities of all thoſe
parts; whereby the benefit Trade, and
the Maſter Trip prove.

Demonſtrated in a Polar Card, wherein are all the maine Seas,
and Ilands, herein mentioned.

With the Author his owne Voyage, being the XVI.
with the opinions and Collections of the moſt famous Ma-
thematicians, and Coſmographers; with a Probabilitie to
prove the ſame by Marine Remonſtrations, compared by the Ebbing and Flowing of the Sea, experimented
with places of our owne Coaſt.

By Captaine LVKE FOXE of _Kingſtone vpon Hull_, Capt.
and Pylot for the Voyage, in his Maieſties Pinnace
the CHARLES.

Printed by his Maieſties Command.

LONDON,
Printed by B.ALSOP and THO.FAVVCET, dwelling in Grubſtre
1635.

THE
STRANGE
AND DANGE-
ROVS VOYAGE OF
Captaine THOMAS IAMES, in
his intended Diſcouery of the Northweſt
Paſſage into the South Sea.

WHEREIN
THE MISERIES INDVRED BOTH
Going, Wintering, Returning; and the Rarities
obſerued, both _Philoſophicall_ and _Mathematicall_,
are related in his Iournall of it.

Publiſhed by His MAIESTIES
command.

To which are added, A Plat or Card for the
Sayling in thoſe Seas.

Diuers little Tables of the Author's, of the Va-
riation of the Compaſſe, &c.

WITH
An Appendix concerning _Longitude_, by Maſter
HENRY GELLIBRAND Aſtronomy Reader
of _Greſham_ Colledge in _London_.

AND
An Aduiſe concerning the Philoſophy of theſe late
Diſcoueryes. By _W. W._

LONDON,
Printed by _Iohn Legatt_, for _Iohn Partridge_.
1 6 3 3.

47

"What! No way! You are kidding!" came out of Sasha immediately. He was truly surprised, but had also been coached by Hugo to deny, deny if anything went wrong.

"Sir, please step away."

Sasha did, but he closely followed the FBI agents into his shop. As he did so, he noted that Herb Trawets had backed himself into a corner, out of the main corridor, but was staring at the James and Foxe books on the counter.

"Mr. Rusti," said Wilson, walking over to that counter and calling him by name, "It is believed that the books here on your table have been stolen from the Woodbridge Heritage Institute. We are going to confiscate them for detailed analysis."

"Again, no way! I bought those books in the open market. I have not stolen anything. That can't be true."

"Mr. Rusti, it may be true that you didn't know they were stolen, but that doesn't matter right now."

"Doesn't matter! What do you mean? *I have not stolen anything!*"

"Sir, would you be willing to tell us how you acquired these books?"

"Certainly, I..."

"Just a moment, sir. You need to be aware that you do not need to answer our questions. You have the right to remain silent. You have the right to consult an attorney. Anything you do say to us could be used in a court of law."

"You are kidding! Reading me my rights? I have done nothing wrong. I will give you all the information you want."

"Fine. I'll ask Agents Barnett and Nelson to gather the information from you."

Wilson stepped back and glanced around the store, hoping to see something relevant but not knowing what to look for. He was careful not to touch or disturb anything. Their search warrant was very narrow in its scope; it related to the Foxe document and their trail of suspicion related to it. The judge had been quite skeptical about the justification and thus had been very specific. Of course, anything that Rusti volunteered was fair game.

Len Nelson stepped forward and started the questions.

"Can you tell us where and when you bought the books?"

"I bought the James a few months ago from a dealer in New England. I bought the Foxe a few weeks ago from an online rare book site."

"How did you find them?"

"I was doing a general scan of books at various sites when I spotted the James. That's how you find books these days. I have systems that scan many dealers' sites, their online catalogues, and new listings on open sites such as Abe Books or Bookfinder. I was getting ready for the Ottawa fair when I saw it as a new listing and I grabbed it. Once I received the book I realized it needed some restoration work to enhance its value and so I didn't take it to Ottawa."

"And, the Foxe?"

"After talking to Mr. Trawets in Ottawa, I realized I had half of the package he was looking for. So, I increased my online scanning to look for a Foxe. Then, a short while ago a hit showed up on my system. It was a new listing and I jumped on it. Then I bundled the two books together, cleaned them up and called Mr. Trawets."

Len looked over at Herb, who just nodded and grimaced slightly, indicating that the story made some sense.

Mark Barnett stepped in. "How much did you pay for the books?"

"I can show you the specific invoices but I recall I paid $144,000 for the James and $135,000 for the Foxe."

"That's a lot of money."

"Earlier Mr. Trawets suggested $400,000 for the pair. That's a big profit in my business."

They continued to talk, seeming to get more relaxed as time passed. Sasha printed out the invoices for the two books.

Then they took a break and the FBI agents huddled in a corner with Herb.

Wilson turned to Herb. "What do you think?"

"It is all credible to me so far, but you will need to follow his sources back. Remember, that's what we expected to do."

Wilson turned back to Sasha. "Mr. Rusti, can we take the James and Foxe books with us for further examination?"

Sasha was surprised by the question. Something didn't seem right. Why were they asking? After a moment he said, "Agent Wilson, I will not just give you my books to take away. I have done nothing wrong and they are mine. If you compel me to turn them over, then I will."

The look on Wilson's face betrayed the quandary he had created.

"That's fine," he said. "My warrant here just specifies the Foxe book; that's all we'll take for now."

Across the street, Hugo Cici had been watching the front of Metro Rare Books from a coffee shop window all morning. He saw Herb Trawets arrive, looking exactly as he expected an old book dealer would. Good!

Then, a short time later, three big men is suits arrived. They might as well as have FBI printed on their backs thought Hugo.

A call to Tony. "It's bad. Feds. Warn people."

48

The next few days were consumed with following up on the seizure of the Foxe journal from Metro Rare Books.

Len Nelson and Herb Trawets immediately examined the Foxe in detail, comparing it with the photos they had taken of the WHI copy. "There is absolutely no doubt this is the same book," said Len.

"I agree," said Herb. "Although there has been some cleaning and trimming, there are dozens of minor marks and flaws that totally match. Along with the pencil marks we made ourselves, it's beyond doubt."

Mark Barnett coordinated a first level background check of Sasha Rusti. Everything seemed normal. He had been in the rare book business for over three decades with no history of any problems. He had a reputation for being a good, mid-level dealer who still maintained a storefront location out of nostalgia. He was recognized in his local circles as being a very astute user of the internet for information searches, which, as one person said, was unusual for someone his age. His personal life seemed unremarkable. He had a nice home and car, all consistent with his business. There were no initial flags for the FBI.

An FBI team out of Boston was sent to visit the dealer that had supplied the James journal a few months earlier. Everything seemed very straightforward. The dealer confirmed selling it to Rusti and had complete documentation of his earlier purchase. It had come from a large private collection in the area, and had documentation to show it had been purchased by the collector decades earlier.

The next step was to visit the dealer who had sold the Foxe to Rusti. The FBI asked Herb Trawets to stay for this next round of activities. He was being paid an advisory fee, and, besides he was keen to see what happened next. His experience and expertise would be critical to judging what they found.

Before going to the dealer, they did some background checking. It was Schuylkill River Books. Even before they started their background checks, Herb said, "I know the name. Schuylkill has been a long-time, established bookseller. It was a very impressive antiquarian bookstore for decades. However, the founder, Jordan Rose, passed away over ten years ago. I had encountered him at various fairs and industry association events, and always liked him. I lost track after he died, but I did hear that his family sold the business. Apparently the new owner shut down the store and has focused on catalogue and internet listings. That's become all too common lately."

Mark Barnett's data scan confirmed what Herb had said. It also identified the current director of the business as Terrance Kent.

Herb didn't know him.

They went to the address for Schuylkill River Books.

It certainly wasn't a bookstore. It was an office in a tower near downtown Philadelphia. There was a plaque with the name beside a door on the third floor. Entering the space, they saw an open area with two people, probably in their twenties, seated at desks, with an array of computer terminals. At the back was an area that was partially enclosed with a waist-high divider and some plants. A man in his forties sat at a desk in that area.

One of the people near the front looked up and frowned slightly. She had never seen four men in business suits walk into their office before. They looked quite imposing.

"Hello," she said, somewhat tentatively. "Can I help you?"

"Yes," said Wilson. "We are agents with the FBI and we need to talk to the person in charge here."

The young woman's eyes widened, in disbelief.

Before she could reply, the man from the back of the office came forward. With a smile, but also a bit of quizzical look, he said, "Hello. How can I help you? What's going on?"

"My name is Agent Wilson with the FBI. These gentlemen and I would like to ask you some questions."

"Sure, I guess. My name is Terrance Kent and I am in charge here. I have a few chairs near my desk that we can use."

When they were settled, he continued, "What do you want to know?"

"Mr. Kent, can you tell us about your business?"

Kent frowned. That seemed like a strange question to start a conversation. But he replied. "We buy and sell used books, mostly using internet listings."

"I understand Schuylkill River Books has been in business for a long time; how long have you been involved?"

"Yes, it used to be quite an upscale bookstore on Main Street. The original owner passed away and I bought it. Over the past years the business has changed and so, over time, we sold off much of the physical inventory that was in the store and evolved into an electronic operation."

"Are there just the three of you that work here?"

"Yes. I must say that I am finding these questions kind of odd. Why are you here?"

"Mr. Kent, we are investigating a book that you sold recently. We're trying to trace its background. I'm trying to understand how your business works."

"The Foxe?"

As he said that, a slight frown and a small intake of air happened but he recovered quickly.

Wilson thought he detected a pause.

"Why do you think we are inquiring about a Foxe book?"

"I remember that book quite well. It was recent and it was one of the most valuable books that we have ever sold. It jumped into my mind."

"Where did you get it?"

"We bought it from another book marketing site; I think it was CARBCo, but I can check. It sold very quickly after we listed it on our site."

"So, you bought it on one web site and sold it on another?" Wilson asked with a note of skepticism.

"That's right. Let me describe how our book world works. People have books to sell, some relatively new, some old. If they are old they always want to believe they are valuable and usually take them to a used bookstore in their area rather than give them to a library or a charity. Those stores still exist almost everywhere, even though there are fewer and fewer over time. Those first-line dealers are usually generalists but they have developed a sense of what might be valuable. Most books they are offered are usually worthless and many of the rest are worth tens or maybe hundreds of dollars. That's their bread and butter.

"If something more valuable surfaces, they will try to do some research but they don't usually have a lot of resources to do that. They will often contact other dealers who have more knowledge and sell it to them at a profit. These second level groups exist in many areas and they basically perform a sorting service. The company I mentioned is one of those, CARBCo, which I think stands for Clearinghouse for Antiquarian and Rare Books Company, a fancy title for a mainline operation. They usually develop general descriptions of the books and list them on their site. Books there are now mostly worth hundreds or a few thousand dollars. They are often linked to Amazon or eBay. Most of their sales are to people who are looking for some specific book or subject.

"More valuable books are often listed on their more proprietary sites where more focused or more professional dealers hunt. That's where we come in.

"Then we repeat that with the higher value books, looking to sell to big collectors or major dealers. We'll provide more elaborate descriptions and usually try to determine a realistic retail value. We use more elaborate sites and sometimes issue catalogues."

Len Nelson then intervened, based on his systems knowledge.

"That seems like a lot of layers. Why so many? Why don't the bigger buyers go directly to the lower sites?"

"I agree that it may seem like a lot of people but it's just a matter of numbers. There are millions of books and thousands of first-line dealers. There are only dozens of top-line dealers, the people who go to the big fairs like New York or big auctions at Christies or Sotheby. The rest of us are doing the filtering in the middle. As technology improves I suspect there will likely be more tightening in the system, but even this system is a long way from the days when low-level book scouts would travel from store to store hoping to find something of value and feeding it into the system.

"A shop like ours can get quite efficient. One of our staff focuses on finding access to other dealers' web sites and catalogues and then generating lists for review. He also manages our own web site. The other person handles the administration. She also does the accounting and banking. I spend almost all of my time scanning those lists for items of interest, buying books and then reselling them. Often there will be direct contact with a seller or a buyer who wants to negotiate."

Mark Barnett then got involved.

"Let's get back to the Foxe book. What were the financial terms?"

Kent squirmed a little. "I don't usually share my buying and selling information with people. That's my whole livelihood; I obviously try to buy low and sell high."

"Mr. Kent, this is an FBI investigation. We are not going to share your information with others. I think your cooperation has been great so far and we would like to keep it in that spirit."

Wilson added, "We do have a warrant for information related to the Foxe but I hope we don't need to use it."

A classic good-cop, bad-cop routine.

"No, no, that's fine. You just need to understand it's sensitive data in my business."

"Fine."

"We spotted the Foxe on the CARBCo site and immediately sensed it was important. You almost never see anything from the 1600s on those sites. Our data scan, which is quite good, picked up one such book being sold at an auction a few years ago for $150,000. Of course, we didn't have detailed comparisons between the book that sold before and the CARBCo one and we don't have direct contacts in that world, but it seemed obvious that it was worth a shot. That's our advantage, we are faster than most others. We snapped it up for $50,000."

"Then you resold the CARBCo Foxe to Metro Rare Books for $135,000?"

"Right, amazing really. That was our asking price, a bit of a discount from that earlier auction. I expected a buyer would negotiate but we got the matching offer very quickly after we listed it. They probably could have got it for one-twenty or less."

This was all consistent with the image of Sasha Rusti being anxious to make the purchase so he could score a big profit from Herb.

They talked for a while longer, but in fact just repeated and reconfirmed what they had already discussed.

As the group was preparing to leave, Terrance Kent said, "You know, you haven't told me why you're asking all these questions about the Foxe. What's going on?"

"Mr. Kent, there's some dispute about the rightful ownership of the book. We are working to establish what's correct."

Kent looked directly at Wilson and then scanned the group. He raised his eyebrow as if to say, "Right, four big-time agents coming to visit me about an old book's history!"

All he said was, "I hope I didn't miss a cache of diamonds or rare stamps in it."

49

The FBI agents and Herb gathered in a nearby coffee shop and compared notes.

Wilson went around the group asking for reactions and for any sense of evasiveness or inconsistency.

Len said, "I thought there was a bit of flinching when Kent volunteered the name of the Foxe book."

"I noticed that too," said Wilson, "but he recovered quickly and his follow-up answers were quite credible."

Herb just said, "What we heard makes some sense. I must admit I didn't know there was so much active internet trading between groups. Times are changing."

Mark added, "Maybe his responses were too good, as if he had rehearsed."

Wilson summed it all up. "That's all quite speculative. So far, we don't have any real leads back to the book thieves or anything else. We knew this was a possibility but I was hoping we would detect something by now."

"So," said Len. "It's on to CARBCo."

The CARBCo office was a hole-in-the-wall space in a rural strip mall. The poorly painted facade and interior layout couldn't conceal that this had probably been a two-man barber shop once upon a time. Now, in the rather barren quarters, was a single person, sitting behind a large table with a couple of laptop computers, a printer-scanner and a telephone. He was maybe thirty. As they entered, he looked up.

"Uh, hi," he said. "Can I help you? Are you looking for directions?"

Obviously he wasn't used to having visitors.

Wilson again took the lead. "We are FBI agents and we want to ask you some questions."

"Oh, OK." Pause. "Is someone in the mall in trouble?"

"No, it's you we need to get some information from. Can you tell us your name and what you do here?"

"I am Andy Dunlap and this is my shop. What do you want to know?" he asked with a bit of a frown.

"You buy and sell old books, is that right?"

"Used books, yeah. Some are very old."

"Where do you get the books?"

"Mostly from independent used bookstores. Sometimes individuals contact me."

"Do you contact them or do they contact you?"

"Both ways. I try to keep in touch with some of the larger stores so they remember me when they have books to sell. Actual deals are usually initiated by them. If they have something that is above their normal range or not likely to be of interest to their retail customers, they look to sell it to someone like me, who can organize it and attract notice from larger dealers. I don't take junk or cheap used modern novels. Generally it has to be worth a couple of hundred dollars or more."

"How do your buyers find you?"

"Most things I list on eBay. I'll place more expensive ones on the Abe Books system and I have a web site of my own where I can also post them."

Everything that Dunlap said was consistent with what they had heard from Terrance Kent.

"Do you remember selling a book by an author named Luke Foxe who was an Arctic explorer?"

"Yeah, I do. That was a bit unusual; I don't get really old books very often. Anyway, it showed up in an email one day with a short description. I went online but couldn't find anything on Abe Books or Bookfinder so I called a dealer I know over in Baltimore and asked him what he knew. He didn't know right away but he had access to some sort of listing of auction sales and told me that a book like it had sold for over $100,000 a few years ago. I was skeptical but at least knew it was likely worth something. So, I bought it and relisted it on my system. I sold it almost immediately. I guess I didn't ask enough."

"What did you pay for the book and what did you sell it for?"

"I bought it for $25,000 and sold it for $50,000. That was a very big day for me"

"Who did you sell it to?"

"It was an online order. I remember because it was a unique name, Schuylkill River Books, but I guess that's not a big anomaly around here."

"Where did you buy it?"

"I remember that too, since it was a big deal. It was Second Reading Books. My contact with them was all online as well."

"Where are they located?"

"I don't know. As I said, everything was online and I made payment by a bank transfer. I suppose you can look them up easily."

50

The group again retreated to a coffee shop and reviewed where they were.

Mark said, "I feel like I'm Alice in Wonderland, spiraling down the rabbit hole."

Len piped in, "We must be nearing the end; the money is getting smaller and smaller. There's not much left for the actual book thief."

Wilson said, "Well onward we go. Let's find Second Reading Books."

Len had his cell phone out and searched online for the dealer.

"I see a general listing; it just says 'Used Books Bought and Sold.' There is no address shown, but there is an email address and a phone number. I'll call them on some pretext and find out where they're located."

Len dialed the number. The phone picked up and he heard a recorded message, "This number is no longer in use. Please redial."

"Damn, it's a discontinued number."

"Try sending an email," said Mark. "People are using the phone less and less."

Len did that, asking a general question about books.

They waited a few minutes, wondering when they would hear back.

It didn't take long. A message popped up on Len's phone. 'Unable to deliver message; destination not found.'

"Oh, boy!" said Wilson. "Let's get to the local FBI office. We need to do some serious stocktaking and get some searches started."

The drive back to the FBI office was somber; everyone was lost in thought.

They gathered in a small conference room.

Wilson took charge. "OK, let's review everything, one step at a time. Herb, I want your reaction to everything we've heard, from Rusti to Kent to Dunlap."

Herb replied, "As I said before, everything we heard generally makes sense, even though it is more technical than I have seen before. However, something doesn't quite ring true. I've been thinking about what Len said earlier about there being a lot of people involved and there not being much money left for the book thief. Perhaps that might be the way things work in the real world of book theft, but our situation is different.

"For all purposes, I put in an order for that specific Foxe book and it turned up. The thief has to be linked somehow to the end-seller; otherwise it doesn't make sense. That means everyone in the chain has to be connected."

"Herb, you are right," said Wilson. We had the premise that the ultimate seller would likely not be involved and that backtracking the book would lead to someone more directly responsible. But the book had to get from the WHI to you without any detours."

"Boy," said Len. "If that's true, they're sure a bunch of good actors. I believed them."

"Maybe too good," said Mark. "You know, no one was flustered and they were all totally consistent. That's not usual. Let's face it, most people get at least a bit disorganized when faced with an FBI agent, let alone the phalanx that we were."

Herb added, "It's also quite surprising, I would even say impossible, that the series of transactions around the Foxe only involved Philadelphia-area dealers, who claim their connections were via online sites. There are thousands of dealers located in every city in the country who could have intervened. It has to have been totally staged."

"If we can get access to all of their records we could potentially establish a pattern of connections between them and maybe link it to more stolen books," said Wilson "I'll work on getting the necessary authorizations. Meanwhile, Len, see what you can find about the demise of Second Reading Books."

"Herb, thank you for all of your help. It has been invaluable. I guess we are now on to systematic police work."

Herb, feeling a little disappointed about not being able to continue with the investigation, but understanding that he could not contribute much more at this point, just said, "You are welcome. I am glad to have been of help. Call me again if there is any more that I can do."

As he departed he couldn't help smiling. Not too long ago he was wondering if the FBI agent at his door was coming to get him; now he was being thanked for being an insider.

51

Agent Wilson appeared in the chambers of Federal District Judge Monica Roman along with an FBI lawyer. He had made a presentation of the circumstances related to the Foxe document and had asked for warrants to obtain the financial and business records of the four entities, Metro Rare Books, Schuylkill River Books, CARBCo and Second Reading Books, even though they had yet to locate the latter.

He summed up his presentation with a bit of philosophy.

"Your Honor, I realize that our case requires some bridge of faith. Occam's razor says that the simplest solutions are more likely to be right than complex ones. Make no more assumptions than necessary. The linear path across these entities is the simple path. It would take a very complex, and highly unlikely set of circumstances, for the Foxe book to get from the WHI to Mr. Trawets in any other way."

Judge Roman looked directly at Wilson, with a small grin.

"Let me sum up what I have heard. You have indications that over a dozen books have been stolen from the Woodbridge Heritage Institute, but have located only one of them, one which you set up to be stolen. You speculate that many more may have been stolen from WHI and other institutions but do not have any proof of that.

"You believe that the stolen books have been used to launder illegal funds, as well as to reap illegal benefits.

"You recovered one book, the Luke Foxe journal, from Metro Rare Books. The proprietor, Alexander Rusti, denies knowing the book was stolen and has provided you with all of the particulars regarding his purchase of it. You have no known instances of any illegal actions by Mr. Rusti.

"You determined that Mr. Rusti bought the book from Schuylkill River Books, where, again, the proprietor, Mr. Terrance Kent, acknowledged the purchase and sale of the book and cooperated with you in providing the particulars. Again, you have no known infractions by him.

"The same story basically applies to Mr. Andrew Dunlap of CARBCo, who sold the book to Mr. Kent. You have been unable to locate Second Reading Books, who provided the book to Mr. Dunlap.

"You have concluded that because the book was stolen from WHI and was offered to your agent, Mr Trawets, there must be a link between all of those entities that entails theft and illegal profits from that theft. Therefore you are requesting warrants to search the premises and to seize the records of those businesses and of their proprietors.

"Is that a fair summary?"

"Yes, Your Honor," replied Wilson.

"Agent Wilson, as you and your counsel well know, I am quite sympathetic to the difficulties that law enforcement officials have with legal process at times and try to be supportive. I might even suggest that it might be the reason you brought this petition to me. However, in this case I cannot grant your request. Everything is too speculative. You have not shown any real link between the entities other than this one book. You have not shown any reason to be suspicious of these people other than their link to this one book, for which they have provided a plausible explanation. Your comments about money laundering are purely hypothetical.

"I am sure that you believe that your premises are true, based on the chain of events and the logic you provided me, but that is not enough. Our laws and practices regarding the Fourth Amendment that prohibits any search or seizure without a warrant based on probable cause demands a higher standard.

"Even if I granted your request, I suspect a good defense lawyer could make the case it was inappropriate and void any information that you uncovered. I can visualize some lawyer arguing that this would be the equivalent of a warrant to search his grandmother's house because she sold a used copy of a John Sanford novel to a used bookstore that had overcharged some customer. Neither of us need that.

"Mr. Wilson, I know Occam's razor. I suspect a modern marketing expert would just say, "Focus: keep your eye on the ball," or something like that. But, I also know our Constitution. Bring me something more and I will reconsider my decision."

"Thank you, Your Honor."

52

Sasha Rusti sat at his bookstore desk and took stock of his situation one more time. It was late Friday afternoon.

Just days earlier he had been preparing to make a huge deal. He recalled the rush he felt when Herb Trawets arrived. How quickly it changed when the FBI turned up.

He had prepared for that eventuality with Hugo's prompting. 'Deny knowledge, be calm and cooperate' were the buzzwords. Hugo had told him to visualize them on the FBI agent's forehead every time he spoke.

Of course, they left with the Foxe. There went the money.

As soon as the FBI agents left, he had called Hugo. He didn't know that Hugo had been watching when the FBI agents arrived and had initiated warnings to the others down the line about what was coming.

Since nothing more had happened over the past couple of days, he assumed that those stops went fine as well. Otherwise Hugo would have let him know. He presumed he would see Hugo at the pub later and get an update.

Hugo was getting ready to make his Friday rounds. It had been a hectic week. As soon as he saw the FBI enter Sasha's shop he had called Tony, and they had contacted Terrance Kent and Andy Dunlap. For two days he held his breath, but nothing happened. Surely the FBI wasn't just going to walk away after one visit with the dealers. The guys had obviously done well but who knows what would happen over time. He could only coach them so much. He hoped he had buried the Second Reading site well enough.

Tony had seethed all week. He knew they shouldn't have gone for the Foxe. He had told Sasha that, even talking about hogs and pigs. He had let himself get talked into it; his bad. And then that book picker, Dennis, had agreed. He had to admit that part worked well. Dennis was smart.

Alberto was a bit concerned. Tony had let him know that the caper had failed. The Feds had the book. If they could trace it back to Dennis, they could find him. But he knew he was a small cog; he could disappear to Miami or Vegas.

Franklin's Fate

Dennis was becoming a bit of a problem. He kept asking when he would get his money. The answer was always when the book got disposed of. That wasn't going to happen now. When should he tell Dennis?

They all waited to see what would happen next.

BOOK SIX

The Renewal

53

Agent Wilson returned to Washington and again met with Director Sybil Stephens.

"Director, we are at a bit of an impasse. I had hoped that gaining access to the records of those bookdealers would provide us with a breakthrough. We don't have any current active leads."

"Are you recommending that we suspend the investigation?"

"I am torn about that. As you were aware, I was somewhat skeptical when we started this investigation after the fake books were discovered and the thefts from the Carnegie were uncovered. I wasn't sure there really was a bigger problem, and I didn't see a huge money-laundering issue.

"Now, although we don't have much more hard data, I do sense there is something larger in play. However, it's also frustrating that the victims, the institutions, are reluctant participants."

"What would you do next?"

"That's the hard question. We would need to start back with the basics. That means a lot of legwork: reviewing records, doing more detailed background checks, maybe even surveillance. It would take resources. Is it worth it?"

"And, your answer is.?"

"I hate to give up. I recommend that I go back there with Mark Barnett and that we recruit a couple of agents from the Philadelphia office. We'll start digging deeper. If we don't get some success in a couple of weeks, we can reevaluate."

"OK, I agree."

Sybil Stephens was glad she didn't need to order Wilson to carry on. She was not going to let this go easily. She had been dogged about it ever since President Cartwright's millions had disappeared into the void.

54

Agents Wilson and Barnett drove to Philadelphia. They met up with Agents Karl Kolby and Ernie Haas, the agents who had helped with background checks at the WHI earlier.

After bringing them up to date on the more recent events, Wilson parceled out initial assignments.

Wilson would go back to the WHI and meet with Director Rhonda Wright again. They needed more cooperation. He would also go over to Baltimore and meet with the head of the Memorial Library. They had reported a couple of missing books, but the FBI hadn't followed up in the midst of all the WHI activity.

Karl Kolby would look harder at the key WHI staff members.

Mark Barnett would dig deeper into the public records of the bookdealers they had uncovered in the Foxe chain.

Ernie Haas would look into the individuals at those organizations.

They decided that they would not go back to the bookdealers yet.

"Let's keep them guessing," said Wilson.

Wilson called Rhonda Wright and they agree to meet that afternoon for a late lunch at a bistro a mile or so from the WHI. That should avoid anyone spotting them.

"Agent Wilson, I am certainly curious about what you have to tell me. Did you get our book back?"

Wilson smiled. Wright was still more focused on her book than on the thief.

"Yes, we have the book."

"Great. And where did that lead you? Have you found a trail back? That was the plan, right?"

"That part is still in progress. The culprits created a complex series of transactions. That's why I wanted to talk with you again."

"How so?"

"First, has anyone else noticed that the Foxe is missing? It has been many weeks."

"No. As we've discussed before, that is not unusual. Most of our books are not looked for very often."

"Right. Since you discovered it missing, have you had any more thoughts about who might have taken it?"

"Lots of thinking; no conclusions. I still can't visualize anyone taking it, but I do know it happened. I did scan the security reports for the days before the book disappeared. Remember, I did see the book there in a midweek visit and it was gone the next Monday. Over those five days no staff members took out any recorded packages. Not surprising; it was summer and people have better things to do with their weekends."

"Have you had any more thought about how the book disappeared the first time for a few days? Now that we know it was actually stolen, the more likely it is that the first event was a bit of a dry run to see who noticed."

"No. Anyone could move a book around on the shelves, if that's what happened."

"Dr. Wright," Wilson said more formally. "You have been robbed of valuable books. What else can you do to help us find the thief?"

"I guess that's your job; you are the expert."

"OK, thanks."

"When will we get our book back?"

"Certainly not soon. We need it for evidence. Also, we don't really know how informed your thief will be about what happened. There are many people involved and the thief is only the first link in the chain. Maybe the thief doesn't know we found it. Let's not be the ones to let that knowledge escape."

The next day, Wilson drove from Philadelphia to Baltimore, about a two hour drive. He had called ahead to arrange a meeting with the Chief Librarian at the Baltimore Memorial Library, Greta Parker.

Once seated, he said, somewhat exaggerating, "I realize that this is a much delayed reply to the note you sent to the ARBC a few months ago, but we have had a lot of items to follow up."

"I understand. We only reported a few books missing in response to their Alert Notice, but, in fact, we weren't sure. It's hard to have complete inventory control here. There are many books and many people in and out."

"Was there anything special about those books?"

"I can't say so. We don't have that many books about the Arctic, mostly donated ones. For some reason we have more about the Antarctic, maybe because Shackleton was a more recent, dramatic, historical figure.

The books were of value, but not extravagantly so. I can give you their descriptions from our files."

"Have you checked to see if other books are missing?"

Greta Parker looked at him as if he was demented.

"Do you mean, 'Did we check out our total inventory of hundreds of thousand books because three books were missing'? No."

"Have you tried to determine who might have taken the books?"

"Not really. We're a big organization with a lot of employees and many visitors every day. I could have probably carried the books out in my handbag if I tried,"

Wilson realized that this was a dead end. Like most institutions, the problem was trivial compared to the effort to fix it.

As he left the office, he didn't notice a woman staring after him. She was Francine Dumont, a book technologist in the library. She was also one of Alberto's book pickers.

She didn't know why, but the Chief Librarian's visitor had caught her attention. Perhaps it was his posture and stride or singular focus; he didn't look like a typical library visitor. She would tell Alberto about him.

55

Mark Barnett made use of the internet, but also visited the state corporate registry offices and contacted a couple of web domain management groups.

Metro Rare Books had a straightforward history. It had been started by Ernest Markham many decades ago and had been taken over by Alexander Rusti about twenty-five years ago. The firm was a member of various bookseller and business associations. It didn't have a high profile but any references that Mark found were positive.

Schuylkill River Books had a similar profile. It had been established years ago by Jordan Rose and acquired over ten years ago by Terrance Kent. It didn't appear to be active in any associations and online references were few.

CARBCo had been incorporated about ten years earlier. It had been organized by a small local law firm. Its name had been registered by Go Daddy. Andrew Dunlap was listed as the General Manager. It had no noticeable profile other than its own website, which was quite presentable.

Second Reading Books was essentially a nonentity. It had been simply registered, similar to CARBCO, ten years ago. However, unlike CARBCo that had an actual business address, its registered address was just a postal box in a community outlet. It had listed a website but that had been closed down a few weeks earlier. The registered President was a person named Christian Jones whose address was shown as the same as the business. Mark could not find any other reference or information about him. It was a total dead end.

Ernie Haas conducted a parallel search for information about the people rather than the companies.

Alexander Rusti seemed as solid in his reputation as his store. He had a nice home in an established neighborhood. He drove a Mercedes sedan. Everything seemed consistent with his business success.

Terrance Kent had an administration background, having worked for a technology service company earlier. His background fitted the business model of Schuylkill River Books that focused on internet sales. Ernie could not find any association with the book business in his history, which seemed a bit unusual. His personal profile was lower key than Rusti but nothing stood out to Ernie.

Franklin's Fate

Andy Dunlap was the youngest of them all, now in his mid-thirties. That meant that when he started CARBCo he was in his early twenties, which also seemed a little unusual. He had graduated from a midlevel business school that had focused on financial and technical skills. He had a reputation with the few contacts that Ernie could find as a bit of an introverted nerd, quite consistent with the office setup and the business.

Karl Kolby reviewed the files on the WHI staff people again. They had conducted a first level review when it was first discovered that the Arctic books were missing. He worked on extending the scope of the background checks and adding details. At first, nothing significantly new seemed to surface.

56

The group reconvened three days after their first meeting to compare notes and decide what to do next.

Wilson, Barnett and Haas gathered in the conference room. Kolby was late but they went forward anyway. Being punctual was an FBI trait, but so was the presumption by the others that Kolby's absence was for a good reason.

After they heard each other's report, Wilson summed up.

"We haven't had any real breakout yet. The information we've gathered so far seems to confirm rather than contradict the stories we heard from the various dealers, and there is no lead back to the WHI or a book thief. The only slight anomaly is that Terrance Kent and Andy Dunlap seemed to appear out of nowhere into the book business, although their general skills were appropriate."

"What should we do next?" asked Mark Barnett.

"We could go another level deeper into our checks on the dealers. Find old friends or family members. See if we can make any connection between them or with someone in common."

"Should we go back and talk to them again?" asked Ernie Haas. "Maybe Karl and I could go next time, just to get another perspective."

"Another visit should happen alright; I was just hoping we would have something in hand to shake someone up. I suspect they are wondering why we haven't been back."

At that moment, Karl Kolby came into the conference room.

He didn't apologize for being late or even say anything initially. Then he broke into a big smile and said, "I have something. Dennis Davis does not have a sister."

After a reasonable pause, and with questioning frowns appearing on foreheads, Mark said, "What? What are you talking about?"

Karl elaborated. "I was expanding the background check on the WHI people. Naturally, I constantly referred back to the notes we took when we did the initial checks. I was checking the bios of the people in more detail, hoping to come up with some follow-up ideas. When I got to a profile on Dennis Davis, it showed he was born in Ohio and had gone to Ohio State for a bachelor's degree in English history and then came to the University of Pennsylvania for a master's degree in library science before joining the WHI, things we already knew. But this profile also included some personal data. It named his parents and showed no siblings. I checked other sources and confirmed that."

Wilson was getting impatient. "So what if he doesn't have a sister?"

"Ernie will remember. When we did the first background check we were trying to determine whether any of the people seemed to be living above their means, as a possible indicator of suspicious income. When we were asking around, a couple of people told us that Dennis Davis was a relatively staid guy, whose only travels were an annual visit to his sister in Florida.

"He doesn't have a sister. Where does he really go?"

Wilson contemplated this information.

"It's thin, but it's our first lead. Great work."

"What should we do next?"

"We definitely don't want to alert him to our suspicions yet. We'll stay away from WHI for now. Mark, start looking for any information you can find about where Davis really goes on vacation. Karl and Ernie, set up some careful surveillance on him. Let's learn more about his habits. I'll dig further back into his history looking for any other leads."

57

Mark contemplated how he could check Dennis Davis's vacation history without raising any alarms.

Even assuming he actually went to Florida, that's a big place with millions of visitors each year.

It was probably safe to eliminate any simple vacations like renting a cottage on the beach in Lauderdale or Naples. Things like that would be easy for Davis to explain; why would he hide something like that?

They had to assume that he had large sums to spend and wanted to hide that. Still, there were lots of upscale places.

Presumably he has been doing this for years. Would he do something different each time or have settled into a routine? He had a personal profile that said he was a relatively conservative, laid-back guy. That would suggest a routine. Besides, if there wasn't a routine, Mark had no hope of finding his history.

The judge had clearly said they didn't have sufficient evidence to justify a warrant to obtain his phone and credit card information. They couldn't compromise the integrity of any charges they might be laying in the future.

Mark did an online search for Five-star Florida Resorts; that seemed like a place to start. There were about 100 listed. That was daunting, but manageable. After all, most detective work really was slogging after details.

He developed an approach. He would call the reservations office at a resort and explain that he was organizing a surprise celebration party for his good friend Dennis Davis. A group of his friends wanted to organize a group event. He understood that Dennis was a frequent visitor at that resort and perhaps they could help him do that. Did they have any information on the specific type of accommodations or activities that Dennis liked to do?

A few people resisted giving out any information on principle. Most were willing to look for that type of data once he convinced them he really didn't want anything too personal. Besides, they sensed a large booking in the offing.

After thirty phone calls he had found nothing and was becoming discouraged. He took a lunch break.

Sitting at a table in a local deli, he looked out the window at a busy street. There was a large billboard on the side of a building across the street. Its headline said "Going to Florida? Go Beyond! Cruise the Seas."

Mark immediately reacted. Of course. That was as likely as a resort and maybe more so; it could be routinized and still offer variety.

Back in the office, he suspended his calls to resorts and checked out cruises. There were almost a hundred ships that sailed out of Florida but only about twenty major cruise lines. That seemed doable.

He started down the list alphabetically. His fifth call was to Clear Seas Sailing.

"Clear Seas Sailing reservations. How may I help you?"

"Hello, my name is Jack Smith. I'm looking to organize a group vacation. We're celebrating a big event for our friend Dennis Davis and we want to surprise him. I understand he has been a good customer of yours. I was hoping that you could recommend something different from what he's already done."

"Oh, that sounds exciting. How many of you will there be?"

"I don't know for sure yet, at least seven rooms, likely more."

"Your friend is Dennis Davis?"

"Yes, from Philadelphia."

"Let me see. Oh, yes, Mr. Davis is a good customer. He has platinum status."

"Platinum?"

"That just means that he has taken ten or more high-end cruises."

"Oh, great. Where hasn't he been?"

"Well, most of our cruises stop at a number of ports. Some cruises make a circular trip and return to where they started. Other cruises just go in one direction and the passenger either books a second cruise back or just flies back from the final destination. Mr. Davis has done all of those things. I could try to search out something new for him and get back to you."

"Maybe I should just get Dennis into a general conversation and carefully ask him what he would like to do next. That's probably easiest and I don't think it would alert him to anything."

"That sounds good. Can I mail you some catalogues that show all of our cruises and the different options of room types and onshore excursions?"

"That's probably not necessary yet. I can find much of that on your internet site. We can get into the details once we have a basic plan."

"OK. Call again if you have any more questions or when you're ready to proceed."

"I will. Thank you."

"Thank you for calling Clear Seas Sailing."

Mark hung up.

"Eureka."

58

Dennis Davis was at his local pub and was frustrated. Alberto was giving him the runaround. He had worked hard and taken a big risk in getting the Foxe book. Alberto owed him $40,000. That was a lot of money for Dennis, more than he got most years from Alberto. But things had stopped. His annual cruise was in jeopardy. He knew he would see Alberto again soon; although he wasn't here tonight. He would push him again.

Dennis was at the pub again a couple of days later. When he was on his second beer, he saw Alberto walk in.

Alberto's first stop was at a table in the far corner where Joe, the bookie, was working over some papers. They chatted for a few minutes and then Alberto came over to Dennis's table.

"Hey," he said.

"Alberto, where have you been? I've been expecting to see you."

"I know. I know. Be patient, things take time."

Tony had told Alberto to keep Dennis in the dark about losing the book. They didn't know how he would react and they might need to use him again. Stalling was the plan.

"Be patient! Enough already. I went out on a limb. You owe me," he said, steadily raising his voice.

"Calm down. Be cool. I'll talk to my boss again."

Then Alberto got up and, with a small wave to Joe, left.

Neither Dennis nor Alberto had paid any attention to the fellow seated by himself at a table against the wall near the front of the bar. He had wandered in shortly after Dennis and had been nursing a beer while pretending to check his cell phone. In fact, he had taken a few photos with his phone.

Karl had been following Dennis since he left work. He and Ernie had been on his trail off and on for a few days. In reality, Dennis led a pretty simple life; they hadn't seen much. A couple of days earlier Ernie had followed Dennis into this same pub but didn't see much of anything to report. He did note that there was one fellow in the bar, who people called Joe, who seemed to be a bookie. Joe and Dennis did not interact. Spotting Joe was instinctive for an agent with Ernie's experience.

This evening, Karl had again easily picked out Joe when he got settled, but didn't think much of it.

After a while, another fellow entered the bar and joined Joe at his table in the back corner. Out of habit, and perhaps boredom, Karl snapped a couple of pictures.

Then things got more interesting. The newly-arrived fellow got up and went over to Dennis's table and sat down.

They seemed to get into an intense discussion right from the start, although Karl could not hear much. At one point Dennis did speak up a bit louder and Karl picked up "...you owe me."

The newcomer left very shortly thereafter. He hadn't stayed long, but long enough for Karl to get a couple more pictures.

After following Dennis home, Karl went back to the office where he downloaded his photos into an FBI photo database. Both people came up, with limited information.

Joseph Salieri had been arrested a couple of times for minor offences, illegal gambling and a couple of assaults. He had paid some fines and put on some periods of probation and community service, no jail time.

Alberto Danza had been arrested a couple of times for assault and battery but had never gone to trial. The file just said charges were dropped due to lack of evidence.

The next morning, Karl called Randy Stockton, an agent who was more regularly involved with gambling, extortion and other street crimes, often linked to organized crime groups.

"What do you know about two guys named Joseph Salieri and Alberto Danza?"

"Slightly familiar. Let me check my files for a minute."

"Sure."

"OK. Got it. Salieri is a low-level guy who works the street, mostly taking bets and doing some follow-up pressure on people who don't pay their debts. Danza is a bit more of an unknown. He started as a driver and errand runner in his group but seems to have moved up and become less visible, probably doing more circumspect enforcement."

"What group are they associated with?"

"Their leader is a fellow named Antonio Esposito, Tony to most."

"Is he a big player?"

"He's in charge of a lot of those low-level activities. You know, organized crime has changed a lot over the past decade or more. The big boys focus on things like drugs, and fighting off outsiders like the Colombians, Mexicans and Asians. These other activities are sort of farmed out to other groups like Esposito's. To be sure, he will be paying some form of license fee or royalty to the big boys."

59

They again convened in the conference room.

Wilson led off. "I did a deeper look into the life and family of Dennis Davis, but nothing new surfaced that seems relevant."

Mark said, "I was able to confirm that he has taken a lot of cruises out of Florida, expensive ones. He has money to spend."

Karl said, "Ernie and I have followed Davis for a few days. Everything was a non-event until last night. At his local pub, he had a brief conversation with a fellow that we have since identified as being part of a local crime group. I overheard Davis say 'You owe me.'"

They all took a minute to absorb what they had learned.

Wilson said, "It's certainly getting more likely that Dennis Davis is our man, but none of this actually links him to stolen books. It's still circumstantial. A good lawyer, or skeptical judge, could just say he was a lucky bettor."

Mark asked, "Now that we have a stronger indication that the thief is Davis, should we go back to WHI and have the Director dig deeper into his behavior?"

"Not yet. We can't let our suspicions get back to him in any way. That would just alert everyone else up the chain."

"Then what?"

"If we think of Davis and the book theft as the tail of the snake, let's go back to the head and see if we can make any connection. Mr. Rusti must be wondering where we've been."

"If we can fluster him somehow, then perhaps if we follow him for a while we'll get another break."

"We can do the good-guy, bad-guy routine with him."

"It's worth a try."

Just then, quite coincidentally, Wilson's phone rang. The screen showed Herb Trawets was calling.

Wilson shrugged and answered it.

"Herb, Wilson here. How are you?"

"Agent Wilson, I had to call you this morning; remember it's early out here in California. I have something I want to share with you."

"What's that, Herb?"

"I've done a lot of thinking about our activities together since I got home. I can't get it out of my mind actually.

"Anyway, as I've replayed the conversations that we had with the dealers in my mind, something didn't seem right but I couldn't figure what. Last night, I was watching a rerun of the old movie *All the President's Men,* and when Dustin Hoffman, playing Carl Bernstein, was told by Deep Throat to 'Follow the money,' it hit me."

"What hit you, Herb?" Meaning 'get to the point.'

"The money. They didn't ask about the money. That's not normal. Sure, Sasha Rusti would immediately deny he knew anything about the book being stolen when faced with the FBI, but then he didn't say anything about his money. He had paid $135,000 for the book. He would want that back. He would want to know what the FBI was going to do.

"No, he just let us take the book away. And, when we got to Schuylkill River Books, Terrance Kent didn't talk about Rusti or the money either. You hadn't told Rusti not to contact anyone. Maybe you should have, but you didn't. Why hadn't Rusti called him asking for his money back?

"Money is what this is all about. Bookdealers face tight margins, even if total values are high. Rusti didn't act right. Quite unnatural, actually."

"Herb, that is important. We will be able put that information to good use. Thanks, so much."

"Great. Call me anytime if you need anything else. I miss being involved."

60

Wilson and Barnett arrived at Metro Rare Books just after lunch time.

Sasha Rusti looked up when they entered, showing no reaction. They had not called ahead but it appeared he was expecting them, at least sometime.

"Mr. Rusti, we have some more questions," started Wilson.

"Fine. What have you done with my book?"

"Sir, we told you. The Foxe was stolen. We have it in safe custody as we investigate its theft."

"As you told me, sure. You took my book away with some legal document. Where is your proof that it was stolen? Give me some better reason why you took my book away."

"It's an investigation in progress. We can't divulge any more now."

"OK. What are your questions?"

"I will just remind you of our earlier advisory comments about your rights."

"Sure."

"I want to be sure we are clear. You don't need to answer our questions, but if you do, you must tell the truth. Remember, Martha Stewart didn't go to jail for insider trading; she went there for lying to the FBI investigators."

"OK," with a slight hesitation.

"Tell us again the details of your purchase of the Foxe."

"No, enough already. I told you how I found it and where I bought it. I gave you the name of the seller and provided copies of the invoice and the bank transfer. What more do you want?"

"Boy," thought Wilson. They had come to question Rusti and were going to use the bad-good strategy on him. He was doing a one-man version of the bad-good on them. He had obviously prepared for their return visit.

Mark Barnett stepped in, going to play the good-cop role.

"Mr. Rusti, We appreciate all of that. Indulge me a minute. As we try to trace the origins of the stolen book, we need to start with you. That's obvious. We appreciate everything you have given us

"We have talked with Schuylkill River Books and they have a similar story of buying and selling the book online. We know that is normal these days."

Rusti nodded slightly.

"What did Terrance Kent say when you asked for your money back on the stolen book purchase?"

"Who? What?"

"Surely you went back to him to recover your money. $135,000 wasn't it? What did Kent say?"

For the first time, Sasha Rusti paused. He had made a big mistake. But, relatively quickly, he recovered.

"I haven't contacted them yet. You said it was a stolen book. I didn't want to interfere with whatever you were going to do as a follow-up."

"Did we ask you to avoid contacting Schuylkill River Books?"

"No, I guess not. I just took that as a given."

"Right," said Mark Barnett.

Then Wilson stepped back in, on a whim.

"When did you last talk with Terrance Kent?"

"I don't remember talking with him for a long time. My purchase was done online. Remember, I jumped at the sighting of the Foxe. I was looking to pair it with the James for dealing with Herb Trawets."

After a few more back-and-forth details, the FBI agents left.

Sasha Rusti let out a big sigh.

He had been prepared for their return but they had caught him out about the money. He hadn't thought of that. He should have called Terrance Kent after the first time the FBI came and took the Foxe, creating a credible action in support of his claim of ignorance about the book being stolen. He believed that he had recovered well but wasn't sure. He needed to talk to Hugo.

Wilson and Barnett stayed silent until they had driven away.

"Maybe we surprised him about the money, but he was fast with his recovery."

"Maybe. The Herb Trawets info sure helped. Let's see what Kolby and Haas can learn by watching him for a while."

61

Kolby and Haas set up a routine between them to follow Rusti. They had all decided that this was a higher priority than spending further time on Dennis Davis for now. Their project still didn't justify more resources.

As with Davis, Rusti didn't have that much activity most of the time, moving between his bookstore, his home, and carrying out routine chores. Karl Kolby read novels on his iPhone. Ernie Haas was more of an online puzzle person.

Karl was on watch Friday evening when Sasha Rusti went to his local pub, the Heath and Heather. As was the routine for this type of situation, Karl followed him in after a brief pause and set himself up at a table against a wall to observe.

Everything looked quite normal for a Friday evening pub. Then, after a short while, a large fellow came in and started to work his way around the room. Many people seemed to know him and often called him "Big." It soon became obvious to Karl that the newcomer was taking bets.

"Oh my god," he thought. "This is like the stakeout of Dennis Davis across the city all over again. Could this guy actually connect up with Rusti?"

Lo and behold, as a novelist would say, that's exactly what happened. After making his rounds, Mr. Big joined Sasha Rusti at his table.

They talked in low tones for a brief time. Karl couldn't overhear anything. Then, with a nod to Rusti and a low key wave to the other people in the room, he left.

Of course Karl had captured a few photos.

Again, back at the office, he scanned the photos into the FBI system and got a hit.

Hugo Cici. Known crime group associate. Minor arrests for gambling-related activities, none of which attracted anything more than fines. The file had a cryptic note from some past investigator: "maybe more senior."

As he had done with the earlier information, the next morning he called his contact in the organized crime group.

"Hi again, Randy. I need some more info. What do you know about a guy named Hugo Cici?"

"Wow. Two calls from you in a few days and you're digging into Tony Esposito's world again. Do you want our help, or do you want my job?" he said with a laugh.

"Neither right now. Just some information."

"Hugo Cici is a bit of an enigma for us. He's called 'Big,' which might just relate to his name and size, but in these groups names sometimes mean more. He hasn't been caught in much. He seems to do some bet running, like your earlier fellow, Joe Danza; but it seems like it's more of a cover than his total role. He seems close to Tony Esposito, but we haven't quite figured it out. As I said, he's very involved but we don't really know how."

"If there was a complicated scheme involving thefts, multi-person activities, and maybe money laundering, could this fellow be involved?"

"Now I do think you need my help or want my job. But, yes. Hugo Cici is a real player."

"Thanks. I'll come back again if I need more information, and I'll share more as well."

"OK." The other agent knew the necessary protocols to contain any information related to an investigation.

62

The group meeting the next morning became energized.

Mark Barnett summarized everything.

"We have it. We have connected the tail with the head. Both Dennis Davis at the WHI and our book dealer, Sasha Rusti, have close connections with these gangsters linked to Tony Esposito. That must mean that all of the in-between people are connected as well."

"Right," said Wilson. "We know that but can't prove anything. It's all circumstantial."

"Surely we have enough to get search warrants now."

"Take a pause. When we went for the warrants before, all we knew about was the chain of bookdealers. That was our only point of access for information. If we go there now with searches we will likely find out more about the book path, but what else? And we will have everyone aware and alert to what we're doing.

"Now, we know there's a connection to an organized crime group. When all of this started, we were just presuming there was something bigger. Larger scale thefts. Money laundering. Whatever. It's much more likely now.

"We don't want to end up with just catching Davis for stealing a book and, maybe, some dealers for handling a stolen book. Misdemeanor convictions at the best."

"So, what do we do?"

"I don't know. Everyone, give me some ideas."

A free exchange of ideas took place.

"We'll only get something on the Esposito group if we can get some corroboration from the book people."

"Why should they cooperate when they'll know we don't have much on them and they'll likely be afraid of the real criminals?"

"We need to get more on them, or at least make them think we have more on them. If can actually link them to a bunch of books being stolen and sold, we could get into conspiracy-type charges, which are more serious."

"Then let's try to link them to the Esposito people more strongly than just a couple of encounters in a bar."

"What if we could get their phone records and check for contacts with people like Hugo Cici and Alberto Danza, or even Esposito himself?"

"That's back to the same problem. We don't have enough cause to get a warrant for their records."

"What about going at it backwards. Let's get the phone records of the Esposito people and look for contacts with the dealers."

"That's an idea. Maybe the guys that follow people like Esposito could come up with some other pretext to get their phone records. And, they wouldn't even know we had the information and so the dealers would still be unaware of our activities."

Mark said, "I'll call Randy Stockton again and see what he can get for us."

He did just that.

After he explained what their case was all about, he asked, "So is there any way you can get access to the phone records of at least Cici and Danza and check for contacts with our chain of book people? There are five people that we know about right now. I can give you their numbers."

"Maybe, we have some general surveillance approvals on a number of those guys. But, I must tell you that we never learn much from their phone calls. They are always suspicious and cautious about wiretaps. They don't talk to each other much on the phone."

"We didn't expect to get any actual conversations, just confirmation that they have talked with the dealers. That would give us some useful leverage."

"I'll see what we can get. How far back do you want to go?"

"I really don't know. This could have been going on for years. A few, at least."

"I'll be back to you."

"Thanks, we are sure hoping this will give us some kind of breakthrough."

63

Two days later Mark returned to the FBI group morning meeting with a big smile on his face.

"We hit pay dirt. They are all connected.

"There was a lot of information to sort through, but having specific phone numbers to target made it manageable. My contact, Randy Stockton, was able to get and scan the phone records for Esposito, Cici and Danza for the past five years. There were no connections between Esposito and the book people, but that's not surprising. We know of his connection to the other two and it would be normal for the subordinates to do these things.

"Alberto Danza has had a steady stream of calls with Dennis Davis over the years, about twice a month. They have had more calls over the past six weeks.

"Hugo Cici has been busy with all of the dealers, Alexander Rusti, Terrance Kent, Andrew Dunlop, and even the discontinued number for Second Reading Books until recently. His historic calls with Rusti were similar to Danza's calls with Davis, about twice a month. He talked to the others more often. Then again, in the last few weeks there were quite a few calls.

"It all adds up to a long term pattern of doing business and a recent flurry of activity after we entered the picture."

After an extended discussion about what to do next, Wilson said, "I think we have enough now to get our warrants based on probable cause."

He was right. Judge Monica Roman approved the warrants.

Then they gathered to decide on their tactics.

Wilson started, "If we turn up at the bookdealers with the warrants to see their records about book buying and selling, with a focus on other dealings between the specific entities, they will protest but they can't be really surprised. It's a bit of an obvious action on our part, although they might wonder how we justified the searches. It shouldn't alert them to what we know about the connections to Esposito. We will keep any reference to that for later."

"What do we hope to find?"

"At least a pattern of past dealings between them. Then, who knows?"

"I think we're still looking for haystacks," said Len.

"Maybe big needles," replied Wilson.

"What about Dennis Davis and the WHI? Are we going to confront him?"

"Let's avoid him for now. His only connection is Alberto Danza and we don't want to reveal that. Maybe I'll talk to Director Wright again and see if we can get a link to him via the stolen book, not via Danza," said Wilson.

"Your relationship with Wright has been a bit testy and you've been to the WHI a few times. We don't want Davis to get more alert or suspicious than he already must be. Why don't you get Wilma Watkins to come up from Washington to talk to Wright?"

"Good idea."

The next morning they arrived at the bookdealers' locations, showed the warrants, and started to gather information.

They each had a team of agents and specialists that had been gathered from the Philadelphia office.

Wilson went to Metro Rare Books. Mark Barnett went to Schuylkill River Books. Ernie Haas went to CARBCo.

Sasha Rusti just smiled slightly, not quite a grimace, when Wilson returned to his book store, with a couple of new people.

"Back again, Agent Wilson. What can I do for you today?"

"Hello, Mr. Rusti. We are here to review your records. I have a warrant. These agents are systems and financial specialists."

Sasha and Hugo had talked about this possibility.

"What? What for? All I did was buy a book that you have told me was stolen. I gave you all the information about that."

"We're investigating a major theft. We need to look for any connections of the book's path to you."

"I bought it from Schuylkill River Books, as I told you. In fact, after you last visited, I did contact Terrance Kent and asked about my money. He was sympathetic but not helpful. He, of course, said he didn't know the book had been stolen and had bought it in good faith. He gave me the analogy of someone being caught with counterfeit money. They are out of luck, not whoever gave it to them innocently."

"In any case we need to see your records. In particular, we want to see any other transactions with Schuylkill River Books as well as CARBCo and Second Reading Books."

"I have bought a couple of other things from Schuylkill River. I don't think I know CARBCo or Second Reading."

"Fine. If you can help these agents, I'm sure we can get out of your way faster."

"Sure." This time he definitely said it with a grimace.

At Schuylkill River Books, Mark Barnett had a similar encounter with Terrance Kent.

Kent protested at first, claiming he had explained his purchase and sale of the Foxe. Then he called a lawyer on the phone, explaining what was happening and describing the warrant. Obviously the lawyer told him to cooperate.

In the apparent scheme of things Schuylkill River Books was the winner. They had bought and sold the book in good faith and made a good profit. Of course, it was all artificial in the paper chain that they had all created.

At CARBCo, Andrew Dunlop just shrugged when Ernie Haas presented the warrant. For him, the Foxe had just been another set of data entries.

Obviously there was no place and no one to serve a warrant for Second Reading Books.

64

Over the next couple of days the forensic teams pored over the large volume of material that they found.

Metro Rare Books had bought five books from Schuylkill River Books over the past few years. None of them matched the known missing books at the WHI. No books had been purchased from CARBCo or Second Reading.

Schuylkill River Books had bought over seventy books from CARBCo. Two of them had a title that matched the missing WHI books.

CARBCo had bought almost thirty books from Second Reading Books. One of them matched the WHI list. It was not the same title as either of the books Schuylkill River bought from CARBCo.

Mark Barnett had convened a meeting of the agents who had gathered and compiled the information. They all stared at the various summary tables that had been prepared. Comments flowed freely.

"Well, the Foxe values certainly exceed almost anything else we see on these lists."

"The books CARBCo bought from Second Reading average just a few thousand dollars each. Their sales on to Schuylkill River average under ten thousand dollars."

"In total CARBCo bought less than two hundred books over two thousand dollars over ten years. That doesn't seem like many."

"In that same period Schuylkill River bought about three hundred books over five thousand dollars."

"Look. CARBCo bought most of those more expensive books from just five suppliers. Those five, including Second Reading each supplied twenty-five to thirty-five books each. That's amazingly symmetrical. The other books came in ones and twos from different places."

"Schuylkill River has the same kind of concentration. Three sources, including CARBCo, supplied three-quarters of the expensive books."

"Maybe all those outfits are linked into a cleansing network process. That could explain the concentration."

"Wow. Look at the names of those five suppliers to CARBCo. First Avenue Books. Second Reading Books. Third Base Bookstore. Go Forth and Read. Five Hills Paper. Somebody was too cute."

"Or just wanted an easy memory jog."

"Schuylkill's three big sources are also on a theme. CARBCo, remember, stood for Clearinghouse for Antiquarian and Rare Books Company. The other two are Book Clear-out and Clean the Attic Books. That's really lame."

"I wonder if there's a parallel operation to Schuylkill River Books."

"Look at who CARBCo sold to. They sold seventy books to Schuylkill River and about the same number to Copper River Readings; that's three quarters of their key books and another symmetrical name."

"I just did some arithmetic. If we assume there are the five first-level dealers, the three second-level dealers and the two third-level dealers, and that the sales numbers we have in our known chain are representative, it means we are dealing with four or five hundred books. And, there may be more dealers involved."

"We also have the name of about 300 books. CARBCO bought about 30 from each of the five lower dealers, which makes 150. Schuylkill River bought about 75 books from each of the three middle dealers, which adds another 150 books when we eliminate the CARBCo duplicates."

"At $20,000 per book coming out the top, which is at least the value of the top books coming out of Schuylkill River Books, that's ten million dollars. Probably more."

"Well done, group," said Mark. "I am amazed how much you could deduce from that maze of data in the book sales records. I'll brief Wilson and the others and figure out what we do next. I am sure you'll be back in action again soon."

65

While that analysis was happening, Wilma Watkins arrived from Washington and, after a full briefing by Wilson, arranged to meet with Rhonda Wright.

"Director Wright, thanks for meeting me on such short notice."

"No problem, I am naturally curious to hear what progress you have made about the stolen Foxe."

"The team is learning a great deal. As I think Agent Wilson told you recently, the thieves created an elaborate scheme to get the book to market. It takes time to follow all of the steps."

"So, why are we meeting today?"

"As well as trying to trace back from the book, we continue to try to find any lead about who may have stolen it in the first place."

"Right, but I thought we had tried that before and didn't find anything."

"Well, maybe we have something, or I should say somebody."

"What? Who?"

"Before I get there I must caution you that this is just a lead and we are still investigating. We do not have enough information to charge, even confront anyone. In fact, to preserve the integrity of our investigation we can't have the person know that we are suspicious. So, I am going to ask for your help but it must be kept confidential."

"I understand," Wright said with an anxious look that mixed curiosity with concern.

"We think that your curator, Dennis Davis, could be involved."

"What? Dennis? I find that hard to believe. He's steady and reliable. I even travelled with him to Ottawa recently. He can't be involved. It doesn't make sense."

"Finding an internal culprit is always a surprise and a shock. I understand that. But we do have our suspicions and do need your help."

"What suspicions? What did he do?"

"I'll just say that we have determined that Dennis Davis has been spending money far in excess of what can be explained by his salary."

"Maybe he inherited some money or won the lottery."

"We have checked and are pretty sure that has not happened."

"Well, I am not convinced. What do you want me to do?"

"I am hoping that with a specific focus on Dennis you might be able to figure out how he stole the Foxe. How did he get it out of the WHI? If we could determine that, we could then confront him and hopefully learn where the Foxe went next."

"Where could I start? As I told Agent Wilson last time, no staff members took out any packages in the period between when I last saw the Foxe on the shelf and when it was missing."

"How else do books get out?"

"Sometimes researchers are given permission to borrow books. Again, there is a strict procedure. No such events took place that week; remember, it was around a summer weekend."

"So, what else?"

"What else? Nothing. Well, we do send books out for repair sometimes but the Foxe didn't need fixing. Again, there are strict procedures."

"What are those procedures?"

"Generally, our book restoration technician, Emma Johnston, would determine that a book needed work beyond what she could do. Then, a requisition would be prepared and approved by myself or Katherine Clay; usually Katherine unless it's high cost. Our budgets are limited. Once the paperwork is completed, including the forms for letting a book out, it would be sent to a professional book restorer."

"Who sends it out?"

"I don't know all the details but I expect Emma does that with one of the administrative staff."

"Were any such books sent out in the time frame we are talking about?"

"I don't know. I never checked that."

"Can you check without arousing suspicion?"

"Let me think. It's not something I would normally do. I guess I could make some pretext like curiosity about how much outside work we are doing these days. That's thin but I don't know who would notice."

"Just be sure that Davis is not around."

Rhonda Wright left her office and wandered into the book area. She noted Dennis Davis working over a pile of papers and books at a desk on the far side. She then walked over to the administration desk at the other end of the area. She saw that one of the young staff members, Chelsea Birmingham, was there.

"Hello Chelsea."

"Oh, Director Wright. Hi. Can I help you?"

"Yes, actually. I was curious about how much outside work we're doing these days on book repairs or other projects. I haven't seen a requisition in a long time."

"We don't do much of that these days, that's for sure. I remember sending out a package a few weeks ago, but that's it. Let me check the ledger."

"Thanks."

"Yes, here it is. Four books were sent to Best Bindings in Radnor about a month ago. Katherine Clay signed off on the order."

"Do you have a list of the books?"

"Yes, right here. Take a look."

"OK."

The Luke Foxe was not on the list.

"I guess Emma organized the books and you did the exit forms and wrapped the package," she said almost absentmindedly.

"Actually, not that time. I remember that Dennis Davis helped Emma out; she was busy with a project. He filled out the forms and wrapped the package. All I did was organize the courier. You can see the forms here."

Rhonda stared at the papers. There were the signatures of Katherine Clay on the approval and Dennis Davis on the administrative forms. It was also clearly his writing on the address label; Best Bindings at some Postal Box in Radnor. She noted the alliterative address, 123 Red Rock Road.

"Thanks, Chelsea. That's helpful."

"Sure, anytime."

Returning to her office, she sat heavily in her chair and looked directly at Wilma Watkins who had been waiting.

"Dennis Davis sent out a package of books on the Friday between when I saw the Foxe and it was missing," she said directly, her disbelief now tinged with anger.

"Tell me the details."

She did.

"Well done. Now, you must tell no one. This must be kept absolutely private. We still have a lot of legwork to do."

"Yes," she nodded. Her face was blank.

66

After checking in with Wilson, Wilma Watkins headed out to Radnor and the office of Best Bindings. She had called ahead and talked to Cooper Best, explaining she was doing some reference checks.

Arriving at the address, she found a relatively small office and warehouse space in an industrial park.

Entering, she saw a chaos of tables and numerous stacked containers full of papers and leather pieces. Etching tools were all over the place. Large presses and clamps stood in one corner. The smell was of glues and ink.

There were books stacked randomly throughout the space.

In its chaos it was quite enthralling.

A pleasant fellow with a big smile came across the room and greeted her. He was wearing a heavy workers apron, stained with inks and whatnot.

"Hi," he said. "I'm Cooper. I assume you're Wilma Watkins. Welcome. How can I help you?"

Wilma had not identified herself as FBI.

"Hi, yes. Thanks for the time. You look busy."

"No worries. I guess the good news is that I'm always busy. No work, no income."

Wilma smiled. She immediately liked Cooper and cautiously put aside her concerns that he might be in cahoots with Dennis Davis.

She even laughed internally. She hadn't thought the word *cahoots* in a long time. Crime these days wasn't that quaint.

"I didn't explain myself very much on the phone, but I'm doing a background check on someone who is being considered for an award."

"Sounds good. Who and what do you want to know?"

"Dennis Davis, the curator at the WHI, is being considered for an alumni recognition award from Ohio State University. He graduated from there in English History, and the department wants to recognize people who have gone on to good careers. Not to downplay the importance, but they have problems convincing students there are more after-graduation opportunities than teaching. Many potential students don't have the speaking skills and social skills necessary to be a successful teacher. There are roles in research and writing. Dennis has done that."

"Why would you be asking me?"

"We want to get some input from people that are not in his inner work circle. We understand he coordinates book restorations with you."

"Well, not really. At the WHI I usually deal with Emma Johnston."

""Oh, we were looking at some recent transactions at WHI and saw that he had worked with you."

"That's right. I guess he was helping Emma. He contacted me about repairs to four books, a nice project for me."

"Did you talk with him much?"

"He called me to organize the work and then I remember he called me to be sure that I got the books."

"Be sure you got the books?"

"Yes, I guess he wasn't sure about the delivery. I don't get many items delivered on a Saturday."

"A Saturday? Delivered? Don't you have a Postal Box or somewhere packages are sent?"

"No. There's no need for that. I have a large delivery portal on the front of the office. Packages can be left easily and securely."

"So, I guess you really can't give me much detail about Dennis."

"Not really. But he seems like a nice fellow, very polite."

"Thanks."

"Back to work."

Wilma sat in her car and thought.

"That just confirms our suspicions."

Then she headed to the address that Rhonda Wright had noted: 123 Red Rock Road. A strip mall. On one building there was a sign for postal boxes and parcel services. Wilma went in.

"Can I help you," asked the clerk behind the counter.

"I hope so. I have a package for Best Bindings and I think they have a box here, but I'm not sure."

"Right. Yes, they do."

"Do they get much mail here? I know they have an office in the city."

"Actually, no. I only recall one package, a large one that didn't fit in the box. The customer picked it up almost as soon as it got here I recall."

Wilma had downloaded some of the background material on her phone so she could reference it if necessary. It included a photo of Davis that Karl had taken in the bar.

"That's my friend who has the box, right?" she asked the clerk.

"Yeah, that's him, but I've only seen him here twice and the rent on the box is about to expire."

67

Wilson gathered the team in the conference room again.

Watkins reported first. "We've figured out how Davis got the Foxe out of the WHI. He packaged it with other books and mailed it to a fake address where he could retrieve it. Quite ingenious actually."

Mark went next. "We've pieced together a network of at least ten entities that have moved books through their system and we can identify about 300 books that they processed. A few are common with the WHI missing books. We have another group of dealers that we could search."

Karl added, "You know, with those 300 book names we could send out another alert to the many institutions. They could easily check for missing books with a list like that. It's not like they have to check tens of thousands of books against their inventory lists."

Wilson intervened. "Slow down. We need to remember our real targets. Even with the swoop in to get the bookdealers records, I don't think they will realize how much we've figured out.

"When we're ready to move, we'll hit the head and the tail of the chain. Probably the Davis end first because it can be explained without referral to the Esposito people. I don't think we need anything more to confront him when we are ready.

"To get to Rusti and have him give us a link to the gang will take a bit more. His connection is the weakest. He only bought a few books from Kent, and none of them were on the WHI list. A few phone calls with Hugo Cici isn't much.

"Here's what I want done now.

"Mark, check out those other dealers but we won't contact them yet."

"Wilma, let's share the list of 300 books with Rhonda Wright at the WHI and Greta Parker at the Baltimore Memorial Library. They've been involved already. If they can confirm more books as being actually missing, we can link the dealers together even more, and hopefully Rusti.

"Karl and Ernie, pick up on the surveillance of Rusti. Maybe there will be more action now that we've stirred things up a bit.

"Oh Mark, also get someone to go back into the phone lists we got for Hugo Cici and Alberto Danza and see if there's any connection to someone on staff at Baltimore Memorial. It would help if we had more than one thief to work on."

BOOK SEVEN

The Surrounding

68

Sasha Rusti was in a quandary. He couldn't decide how serious his situation was and if there was something he should be doing to reduce his risk.

The FBI had been to Metro Rare Books three times over the past couple of weeks. The first time they seized the Foxe. The second time they just seemed to want confirmation of the things he told them the first time. The third time they came with a warrant and took copies of many of his book dealing records.

He thought that he had handled the situation each time reasonably well, but what would happen next. Everyone needed to have the same story, consistently, every time. Hugo did all of the coordination, obviously under the direction of Tony. He needed to talk to them again.

The more he thought about the recent events, the more concerned he became. The FBI didn't just carry out superficial investigations.

He called Hugo.

Two mornings later, again before his bookstore opened, Tony and Hugo turned up.

Tony took the lead.

"Sasha, you must stay calm and not do anything to attract more attention. You seem to have handled everything well so far, as have the others. Your stories are simple and consistent. Just stick to them."

"But the FBI doesn't just quit. They must be suspicious."

"Suspicious? Probably. But they need proof before they can do anything. We made a mistake going after that Foxe book. It seemed suspicious, but that's all in the past. We can't let a small mistake turn into a big problem. Sit tight."

"I don't think it's that easy. The first visit by the FBI was obviously the result of a setup by Herb Trawets to lure the Foxe out from the WHI. Otherwise, how could they identify the book so positively? That is quite a feat. We thought that the action there had settled down after the first discovery of missing Arctic books. Instead, it developed into a very sophisticated bait-and-trap scheme. Only our elaborate chain of transfers has kept them from linking it all together. But they must be trying."

"Of course. But trying isn't doing. You are quite remote from the rest of the action. Even your contact with Terrance Kent at Schuylkill River has been very limited. Don't get any more involved."

"What about your so-called picker at the WHI?"

"What do you mean?"

"Well, if the FBI and Trawets set up the Foxe at the WHI to be stolen, they must have been watching for it to disappear."

Tony was taken aback a bit with that comment. He hadn't thought of that implication.

Hugo stepped in. "I can tell you that there has been no activity around the picker. Besides, he doesn't know anything. He has one contact that takes the books from him. He doesn't know where they go after that. Even his contact has little information about the later stages."

"Right," added Tony. "Even if they caught the book picker somehow, there is no link back to you, Sasha."

"I just want it all to go away."

"The only way that happens is if you do nothing and say nothing. At some point even the FBI is going to decide it has better things to do than chase dead ends over a few stolen books."

"All those books were worth millions. And, that doesn't count all the other money we washed through the system at the same time."

"Chasing the Foxe isn't going to turn up those rabbits."

As they left the bookstore, Tony said to Hugo, "Let's keep away from that guy for a while. Also, go back to Alberto and have him check on the pulse of that picker, Davis."

"Holy Effing Shit!"

Karl Kolby mumbled words that FBI agents probably weren't even allowed to think in the J. Edgar Hoover days.

He and Ernie Haas had been on surveillance duty for a few days. Watching Sasha Rusti was generally boring. He went to his book store relatively early each morning and stayed there most of the day. He hadn't even gone to his local pub the past few evenings.

Then, this morning two fellows turned up at Metro Rare Books shortly after Sasha Rusti arrived. Karl immediately recognized them. One was Hugo Cici, the same fellow he had observed Rusti meeting in the Heath and Heather some time ago. The second one was Tony Esposito, The Boss. Karl had seen his face on various reports recently.

Karl's camera was busy, totally hidden from view in his parked car.

"Big mistake, Tony," was his immediate thought.

69

Wilma Watkins again arranged a meeting with Rhonda Wright.

"Director, we have some more information. We have a list of books that were possibly stolen from institutions such as the WHI. We would like you to check to see if they are supposed to be here and if they are actually here. I know the first time we met you said that such a search would be quite manageable, as compared to trying to cross-check your total collection."

"Yes, that should be easy."

"Of course, we still want our ongoing investigation to be confidential."

"Oh, I'll have to think how to do that. As Director I don't usually drift around the stacks doing inventory checks. Also, I must ask. Do you still think that Dennis Davis is involved?"

"Yes."

"So, the checking can't involve him or be observed by him."

"Right."

"How many books are on your list?"

"About three hundred."

"Three hundred! Do you think we have lost that many books?"

"No. No. It's just a screening list. I have no idea how many you might find missing."

"Well, the first step would be to check our master lists to see if we even have any of the books in our system. Someone typing key words into the data base could likely do that in a few hours. Then checking to see if any of those books are missing from our shelves, depending on how many books were flagged, might take an hour or two. That's likely at least four hours of activity. People might notice."

"Off hours?"

"You mean like a Midnight Skulker? Even then, security watchmen might notice and comment to others. Sunday would probably be best. Staff seldom come in but I do once in a while to get organized for the upcoming week."

"Can you do that?"

"I would sure prefer to have some help. Alone, it could take a lot longer. I don't do extensive data searches much anymore."

"Could I help?"

"You certainly could, but again your presence would be noted by security or anyone else who happened to be in the WHI. What if I ask someone to help me, someone who is above suspicion?"

"In my business, no one is above suspicion."

"I was thinking of the young administrative clerk, Chelsea Birmingham. She is bright and can manipulate the data systems easily. She's a relatively new hire, and so if this problem has been going on for a longer time, it's unlikely she was involved. Plus, she openly shared those shipping papers that identified Dennis Davis."

"Good idea."

Next, Wilma drove to Baltimore and met with Greta Parker.

"Thank you for seeing me."

"No problem. How can I help you?"

"A while ago, my associate, Agent Wilson, visited you about the books you reported missing. I think you explained the difficulty in doing an inventory check in such a large collection with limited resources."

Greta Parker smiled. "If that's what Agent Wilson reported, he is very diplomatic."

Wilma smiled back. "We may have an opportunity to simplify your search." As she had done with Rhonda Wright, she explained the list of possibly-stolen books and the suggestion that they search their records and inventory.

"The problem, of course," Wilma continued, "is that if those books are missing we don't want to alert whoever took them to the fact that we know. Would you have any suspects?"

"Not a clue. I can't imagine it even happening."

"How could you check the list of books against your books? Could it be done off-hours?" Wilma asked, knowing what they were planning at the WHI.

"We're open seven days a week, even into the evenings. I'm thinking that a slow but steady process would likely go unnoticed."

"How would you do it?"

"Probably get a staff technician to help, on some premise. That would avoid the more senior people who, I guess, could be more likely involved."

At that point, there was a buzzing on Wilma's cell phone. She glanced down and saw that the call was from Mark Barnett.

"Please excuse me," she said. "This call is from another agent working on the same case."

"Fine."

"Mark?"

"Wilma, I understand you're in Baltimore."

"Right."

"We got a phone number contact between Alberto Danza and a staff member there."

After she hung up, she said to Greta Parker, "Do you know someone named Francine Dumont?"

"Oh, no. That's the person I was thinking I would ask to help me look for the books on your list."

By the next Monday, Wilma had the feedback from Rhonda Wright and Greta Parker.

Both of their organizations had over one hundred of the three hundred books on the list in their systems, although there were duplicates. They both had over fifty of those books missing.

They were shocked, to say the least. However, they did agree to keep everything confidential for a while, although they would need to brief at least one senior executive and their senior in-house lawyers.

Mark Barnett had carried out his couple of assignments.

As he had passed on to Wilma, the further cross-checking of the phone records of Cici and Danza had found the one Baltimore Memorial link.

His search of the newly-identified bookdealers in the chain of buys-and-sells found that the other first-level organizations had false-front addresses, as had Second Reading Books. The two second-level dealers looked similar to CARBCo. Copper River Readings had all the same characteristics as Schuylkill River Books. As instructed, he hadn't followed up with those.

70

Efrem Wilson gathered everyone together.

Len Nelson had rejoined the process. With his background in data systems, Wilson wanted someone who hadn't been too close to the investigation lately to help them consolidate their position.

They had a fair bit of data, but a lot more hypotheses, collaborating coincidences, and circumstantial conjecture.

Wilma, Mark and Karl had shared their latest learnings. They were all significant. Many books were confirmed missing from the WHI and the Baltimore Memorial Library. Dennis Davis was undoubtedly the book thief at WHI and they had a name at Baltimore Memorial. Tony Esposito and Hugo Cici were spotted meeting with Sasha Rusti.

While everyone discussed and debated their thoughts about all of that, Len drew some diagrams on the white boards in the meeting room. One showed the network of bookdealers, with a side chart showing the WHI and Baltimore Memorial people. The second chart showed all of the confirmed connections between the Esposito gang and the people on the first chart, whether by observed meetings or phone records. It was quite a set of illustrations.

The people in the room were impressed. Their thoughts and comments included: 'Overwhelming;' 'Amazing consolidation of so many pieces;' 'What a jigsaw puzzle we solved;' 'Won't they be surprised;' 'We got them.'

Len then looked at Wilson, who nodded.

"Folks," Len said, "We have diddly-squat. We know more than we did a while ago, but that's still not enough. Maybe we can get Davis for stealing the Foxe, close to a misdemeanor. Everyone else will claim ignorance and innocence. Any money that's superfluous will be attributed to gambling winnings, and thus explain any contacts with the Esposito people. They wouldn't even need an expensive lawyer. Maybe get a few fines or tax bills.

"And who wants to go to trial for a bunch of trivial bookie charges. Hell, the judges and juries could even be sympathetic to the bookies. They're just providing a social service. Besides, they're being driven out of business as gambling becomes legal in most states. The NFL and NHL have teams in Las Vegas. The sports networks are steadily reporting betting odds and promoting fantasy leagues. As far as money laundering goes, we have nothing."

The mood in the room sank. Euphoria became quiet frustration. The case was so obvious. Had they wasted their time? What more could they do? Were the perps going to get away with it all?

Wilson stepped back in.

"We must make a case," he declared.

"We do know now that there is a wide network of organizations that have been involved with hundreds of stolen rare books, worth millions, over many years. It has been coordinated by the Tony Esposito gang. They probably coerced their suppliers. That has all of the necessary ingredients for getting Esposito and his gang on RICO charges.

"As you all know, RICO, the Racketeer Influenced and Corrupt Organization Act, was designed for just these situations. It allows conviction of those people that organize and order criminal activities, even if the actions were actually carried out by others. It even allows for civil actions by aggrieved parties to recover damages. The institutions could sue the gang members."

"I am not sure. How do we make that case in court? As Len said, they have too many loopholes and plausible explanations," said Mark.

Len stood up again and pointed at his diagrams.

"The crossroads of everything is Sasha Rusti. He is the key link between the book world and the Esposito group. If we can get his cooperation and testimony, we can make the RICO case."

"If we can confront him with everything we know, even adding in some speculation, we can convince him that he is facing a long time in jail. He won't want that, with his background and at his age. Then maybe he'll give us what we need," said Wilma.

"But, he'll be afraid of Esposito and his gang and what they might do in retaliation," said Mark.

"Then we offer a deal that includes witness protection; getting Esposito would justify that."

Wilson again spoke up. "I agree. It's our only hope. We need to surround him and squeeze him.

"Mark, work with the legal office to draw up a charge sheet for Rusti.

"Len, consolidate all of our information, both known and speculative, so that we have it handy when we confront him.

"Wilma, organize the search warrants for those other bookdealers and get charges prepared for Dennis Davis and the Esposito group.

Once we have braced Rusti, we will need to move quickly on those other fronts."

Wilson continued, "Actually, I think we should move on Davis right after we move on Rusti. He is the start of the chain and Rusti is the end. He may not be able to give us as much as Rusti about the Esposito activities, but who knows? He has obviously been involved for a long time.

"Also, I am going to call Herb Trawets again. So far, we only have speculation about money laundering. I will ask him for ideas on how we can uncover it in a bookselling system."

71

Wilson called Herb Trawets.

"Herb, it's Efrem Wilson calling. I need your advice."

"Sure, of course. What's happening?"

"We are preparing to move forward on our case, but there is one aspect that I need your help with."

"What's that?"

"When all of the stolen books are sold, the money needs to be accounted for in some fashion. The trail between dealers is part of it, but there needs to be a beginning and an end with payouts to everyone involved. How can extra funds be camouflaged in a book seller's system; for example Sasha Rusti's Metro Rare Books?"

"Let me think for a minute."

"Sure."

Herb Trawets mind raced. The FBI was asking him how money could be laundered by a bookseller. He had done just that with the millions he had swindled out of President Cartwright years earlier. But of course the possible techniques were obvious, and any dealer could describe them.

"Agent Wilson, I can think of two general ways someone could create accounts for extra funds.

"One would be to create a fake purchase and sale of a specific book. It would take some careful paperwork with dummy invoices but in a large business with many transactions they could easily blend in.

"A second way would be to change the invoices on actual book purchases and sales. Discounts are often given in specific deals. The invoices could be doctored to show larger discounts on purchases and smaller discounts on sales so that extra money appears as a profit. Again, the paperwork would be lost in the myriad of activities."

"How could that be detected?"

"In a busy business it would be very difficult. You would need to confirm actual purchases and sales with specific customers and compare them to the invoices in the accounting system. That seems like an overwhelming task, unless you can identify some specific transactions that are suspicious for some other reason."

"OK. Thanks. That information will help me."

72

They were ready.

Early on a Monday morning, the FBI agents knocked on the door of Metro Rare Books. They knew that Sasha Rusti had arrived shortly before.

"Mr. Rusti, we need to talk with you again," said Wilson.

With a surprised and puzzled look on his face, Sasha waved them in.

Agents Efrem Wilson, Wilma Watkins, Len Nelson and Mark Barnett entered.

"You folks are up early," said Sasha as they all sat down.

"Mr. Rusti, we are here today to talk with you about extensive book robberies from many institutes over many years that resulted in large sums of money being realized and laundered through fabricated accounting."

"What? You are kidding. No way."

"Mr. Rusti, again I will repeat to you that you do not have to talk to us but that anything you do say could be used in legal proceedings. You have the right to have legal counsel present at any time. Do you understand?"

"Yes, but I didn't do anything and I don't know what you are talking about."

"Mr. Rusti, I have told you before and I will repeat it again; making a false statement to an FBI agent conducting an investigation is a felony. I am going to take your last statement as a general expression of surprise and a reflex to this situation. Otherwise, you may have already just committed a felony."

Sasha Rusti stared at Wilson.

"I think I need a lawyer."

"Mr. Rusti, as I said, that is your right. If you had said 'I need a lawyer,' I would have to stop talking right now. However, your saying 'I think I need a lawyer,' leaves it open for a minute. Please hear me out before you say anything else."

"OK," very quietly.

"As I said, there have been extensive robberies and large sums of money realized from those thefts. The process has involved a complex web of bookdealers, such as the group involved with your acquisition of the Foxe book. You have been involved in this conspiracy of robberies and money laundering. We are prepared to charge you with those crimes. We also know that a group of criminals, including Tony Esposito and Hugo Cici, have been involved. You have interacted with those people. If you cooperate with us in completing our investigation, it will influence the charges, penalties and sentences that you will face. You know the nature of those people and so you might want to be careful about openly sharing this situation and anything you do."

Sasha's mind froze. He held up his hands, as if to call a time out. He said nothing as his sense of panic subsided and he tried to think through the situation. Obviously he was in big trouble and the FBI had a lot of information. Tony Esposito was a threat to be reckoned with. He needed help.

"I want a lawyer."

"Fine. You can call one now, or, by law, we can arrange to have one appointed."

"Let me think a minute."

Sasha had a lawyer who handled his business affairs but he didn't think he was up to this type of thing. He was just a paper shuffler. He didn't know if a court appointed lawyer would be appropriate. He had a sense they tended to be junior people, but he didn't really know. One of his regular book-buying customers was a very successful lawyer in the city; he was often mentioned in the news. Sasha had sold him many valuable books over the years. He decided to call him.

After a delay of two hours, which itself was amazingly quick for such a high-profile lawyer, Mason Price arrived. Sasha had emphasized that his situation was serious and it involved the FBI.

Sasha and the FBI agents had spent the time in silence, although the agents did browse through the books on display in the store.

After introductions were made, Price asked for time to talk with his client in private.

"Thank you for coming so quickly," said Sasha.

"I am glad that I could respond. Obviously you have some serious issues; there are four FBI agents here."

"Yes. Where should I start?"

"First, let's confirm that you are hiring me to represent you in this situation. That establishes a lawyer-client relationship and thus ensures that our conversations are confidential and protected."

"Yes, I agree."

"So, let's start by your answering some questions. As I said, our conversations are confidential but I don't need to hear everything now. I can't divulge anything you tell me, but neither can I lie or misrepresent anything. Sometimes I might want to speculate or hypothesize with the authorities and so don't want to be limited too soon."

"OK. I guess so."

"What have the FBI agents said to you?"

"They said that there have been major thefts of valuable books organized by criminals and that I have been involved with them in organizing the thefts and selling them for illegal gains."

"Did they say why they believe all of that and give you any evidence to support the charges?"

"No, they were very general. They did name a couple of supposed gangsters that were involved and said that I interacted with them."

"Anything else?"

"I did buy and try to resell a book that was apparently stolen from the Woodbridge Heritage Institute. It was an FBI setup. That's what started all of this. I did show them my buying records for the book from another dealer some time ago. This is the fourth time that the FBI has been in my shop over the last few weeks."

"You didn't contact a lawyer after any of those other visits?"

"No, I didn't think it would come to this."

"What else did they say?"

"That if I cooperated with them it would influence any charges I would face. They implied that they were more interested in pursuing charges against the organized criminals."

"Are you concerned that if they lay charges against you and it all becomes public that you could be in some sort of danger?"

"Yes. And, my reputation and my business will be ruined."

"Let's rejoin the FBI agents. I want to hear what they have to say firsthand. Then we can decide what to do."

When they had reconvened, Mason Price spoke first.

"My client has given me a general overview of the situation. Normally I would advise him to say nothing at this point and I would spend a much longer period of time getting into details, but he has explained that there are some sensitivities involved and time may be important. Thus, I would like to hear firsthand what the FBI is proposing."

Wilson took the lead.

"Mr. Price, over the past many years hundreds of valuable rare books have been stolen from a group of institutions. They were worth millions of dollars. These thefts were organized by a crime group headed by a Mr. Antonio Esposito, in collaboration with your client, Mr. Rusti. The stolen books were liquidated through a network of bookdealers, organized by the same people. The funds were laundered by those transactions and by other activities by the dealers, including Mr. Rusti's firm. We are prepared to charge Mr. Rusti with conspiracy to steal valuable goods and to dispose of those goods for an illegal profit.

"However, in return for Mr. Rusti's full cooperation, we are willing to reduce the charges, assure him that no incarceration will take place and, if he chooses, relocate him to a new location with a new identity, usually referred to as witness protection."

"It sounds to me that your case is based on a lot of hypotheses and speculation. Why should my client cooperate at this point?"

"We have a defined trail of a valuable book that ended up with Mr. Rusti. It was sought out by Mr. Rusti in response to an offer he received directly. We have conclusive evidence that Mr. Rusti met with Mr. Esposito and his associates on many occasions."

"You have a case based on a single stolen book?"

"We have compelling evidence of a long-term pattern of communication, coordination and collusion by Mr. Rusti and the Esposito group."

"What does full cooperation mean?"

"Answer all of our questions fully and truthfully, provide us with any records or documents related to all this, and testify against the other participants."

"How can he do all of that and be assured of his security?"

"We have well-established procedures. Under the RICO regulations, even testimony can be obtained in a secure fashion."

"If we agree to all this, we will need a legal agreement confirming everything."

"In anticipation of this meeting, we have already prepared a legal document with the appropriate sign-offs by the necessary authorities. It becomes effective if it is countersigned by me and your client."

"Have the other people you mentioned been arrested as well?"

"I can't tell you the details. They are imminent."

"I suspect they are dependent on my client's cooperation."

"Somewhat, obviously. But your client's arrest is also imminent."

"Let me see the document."

Wilson passed the paperwork to Price.

"OK. I need some more time with my client. It's lunch hour. Perhaps you can order in some food and we can take a break.

Mason Price and Sasha Rusti went back to Sasha's inner office.

"Well, Sasha, this is quite the situation you are in. You gave me the gist of it all earlier, but now that we've heard the FBI's synopsis, is there anything else to tell me?. Are any of their basic premises demonstrably wrong?"

Sasha replied, very quietly and almost sullenly, "They have it right."

"How could they prove their case against you?"

"I don't know that. I was caught with the one book, the Foxe. I don't know what else they have."

"It's possible that they have a lot of circumstantial evidence and conjecture, but limited hard evidence. We could refuse their offer and fight the charges."

"What's the benefit of that? If they do have enough evidence, I pay fines and likely go to jail for many years. I am too old for that. If I accept the deal I go free. And, even if they don't convict me, I am still vulnerable to whatever Tony Esposito and his gang does. My business would be ruined. There is no win in fighting this. How else can you see it?"

"I seldom advise a client to plead guilty so early in a process. You never know what will unfold. But in this case the penalty for doing so is almost a reward. If that's what you want, I will support it. However, I will test them a bit."

"By the way, hypothetically speaking, if someone did what they have accused you of doing, how much money would be involved?"

"A few million dollars, I guess."

They reconvened with the FBI agents.

"Agent Wilson," started Price, "can you give us more details about your case against my client? We acknowledge Mr. Rusti ended up with the Foxe book, but he has explained that. How can you link him to all of these other allegations?"

"Mr. Price, I am not going to show you everything we have now. As I told you, the book trail is fake and we can prove that. Mr. Rusti has met with Esposito and Cici, and we can prove that. Enough?"

"That seems very circumstantial. We could just be talking about one book, the Foxe. I doubt that a very severe penalty would ensue."

"Mr. Price, we are talking about conspiracy to commit grand theft, receiving stolen property, and general criminal misdemeanors. We are talking about collaborations with known criminals in a RICO situation. This is all very serious for your client."

"Your agreement document talks about reduced charges and no incarceration. What does reduced charges mean? What other penalties will he face?"

"We don't have all of the details yet about the books sales and other money washing. There could be financial penalties."

"That is too open ended. If Mr. Rusti cooperates with you he can't be left financially impoverished."

"What do you suggest?"

"Let's add in that there will be no financial penalties but that he will pay all of his expenses in witness-protection living. You just need to provide the paperwork and logistics."

"That's too much. Mr. Rusti probably cleared huge amounts, millions even. Let's say any penalties will be dependent on his cooperation and the effectiveness of his testimony; with a cap of one million dollars."

Mason Price looked over at Sasha Rusti, who had not said a single word through all of the negotiations. He nodded slightly.

Price said, "We have a deal. Let's sign the papers and you can start your questions."

As they did all of that, Price thought to himself, "I guess my fee for today's work can be full-scale."

73

They sat around the large table in the center of Sasha Rusti's bookstore. Sasha sat at one end, with Mason Price at his side. Wilson sat at the other end with Wilma and Mark on either side. Len managed a video recorder and also a back-up voice recorder.

After a few preliminaries to set the scene for the record, Wilson started. He had decided to be direct and somewhat non-sequential, hoping to gain extra insights and to detect any inconsistencies.

"Mr. Rusti, approximately how many books did your operation steal from major institutions?"

"478."

"What?"

"478. No, it's actually 479. I forgot to add the Foxe."

"You kept track of each book?"

"Yes."

"Do you have a list?"

"Yes, it's on a flash drive in my office."

"OK. We will get back to that. When did the book thefts start?"

"About twelve years ago."

"Was it your idea?"

"No, not at all."

"How did it happen?"

"The short version is that I met Hugo Cici at my local pub. One day he approached me to help him wash some money though my bookstore. After some discussions, we started creating some fake book transactions to cover his money. However, it didn't really come to a lot and he wanted to expand the scale. Then he brought Tony Esposito into my place and they suggested we could make more money by selling stolen books.

"The next thing I know they tell me they can get books from the Woodbridge Heritage Institute. I was asked to suggest a book as a first trial. There is an irony here. I suggested the James. After that, the book thief determined what books to take, up until the last book, the Foxe. Those two much-related journals created the bookends for the whole venture and were the only two that I initiated.

"After the James, a book arrived about once a month. Later, they expanded the operation to cover other institutions."

"You sold those books through your store, Metro Rare Books?"
"A few at first, but that became too risky. My size and profile couldn't handle that volume and quality. So we set up a series of dealers and the stolen books moved through them until they were finally sold to the marketplace."
"You managed all of that?"
"No. I helped set it all up. Hugo Cici and others managed it."
"So the books moved through the system, just like the Foxe book did from Second Reading to CARBCo to Schuylkill River to you?"
"Right."
"You created First Avenue Books, Third Base Books, Go Forth and Read, Five Hills Books, Book Clear Out, Clean the Attic, and Copper River Books as well?"
"Wow, how did you know all that? Yes."
"Where did the books eventually end up?"
"They were all sold into the market. Collectors. Major Dealers. Sometimes regional auctions. Most of that was done by Schuylkill River Books and Copper River Books, but sometimes the other dealers would make a direct sale. The books were listed online, even if only for a short time."
"Who stole the books in the first place?"
"I don't know."
"How can that be?"
"Tony arranged for all that. He claimed his pickers, as he called them, were happy to make some money."
"Do you know a Dennis Davis?"
"No."
Mason Price intervened. "My client meant to say 'not to his knowledge.' He doesn't want to be trapped by your discovering some forgotten contact."
"Fine," said Wilson. "Do you know a Francine Dumont?"
"No, not to my recollection."
"You said the first books came from the WHI, is that right?"
"Yes."
"Did some also come from the Baltimore Memorial Library?"
"Yes. You guys did really dig in."
"Where else did books get taken?"
"There were five places in total. The others were the big libraries in North Washington, Wilmington and Trenton. All in the general region but not too close to each other."
"How was the money split?

"Originally I got twenty percent, but as the operation grew and I was less involved in the details, I got less, maybe fifteen percent on average. The rest went to Tony Esposito and Hugo Cici and whoever else was involved at their end, obviously with some going to the actual thieves. I didn't know those people."

"Do you know an Alberto Danza or a Joe Salieri?"

"No, not to my recollection."

"What about the money laundering. You said that was how it started."

"Early on. After that, I guess Hugo and Tony did it on their own with the various dealers. I wasn't involved with that, although they gave me an annual payment to recognize the original idea."

"How much was that?"

"It varied. Maybe a hundred thousand dollars."

"You didn't launder any money?"

"Well, my own money; the money I got from the stolen books."

"How did you do that?"

"Fake book transactions mostly."

"Also, fake discounts on invoices?"

"Right. You have learned our business pretty well."

"How many times did you meet with Hugo Cici?"

"Over the years? Dozens of times; probably more."

"And Tony Esposito?"

"Not that often. A few times in the early days. Maybe once a year for most of the time. More often lately with the Foxe screw-up."

"Whose idea was it to steal the Foxe?"

"That one's on me. That guy Trawets certainly set everything up well. What a long con that was. It's ironic in a way. Tony didn't want to do it. If he had insisted, none of this would have happened."

The questioning continued for some time, with the other agents asking for clarification of details.

As they concluded, Wilson said to Sasha, "You had better organize yourself as best you can tomorrow. We will have someone monitoring you until tomorrow afternoon, when we will pick you up. Then, for the short term we'll just put you in a major hotel somewhere; you'll be invisible. You will be able to manage business and financial things through our systems for a while without being detected. Just don't show up at your home or here again without clearing everything with us.

"Then start thinking about your new life. Charlotte? Austin? San Diego?"

74

After finishing with Sasha Rusti, Agents Wilson and Watkins headed to the WHI. Director Wright had been alerted to expect them late afternoon and had been asked to find some way to be sure that Dennis Davis would still be there.

First, they met with Wright.

"Director, we have started to round up the people who were involved with the thefts of the books from the WHI. Most of them will be arrested tomorrow. However, we wanted to confront Dennis Davis early. He has been involved for a long time and he may be able to give us additional information about the others."

"OK," she replied with a sigh. "I knew this day was coming. I'm feeling both anger and sadness about everything."

"Can you call Davis to join us?"

"Yes, he has been in the rare book library all afternoon working on his project. I didn't need to do anything to keep him here."

When Dennis Davis entered the room and saw the FBI agents he reacted with a startled look and then, after a brief pause, seemed to just shrug.

Agent Wilson led off. "Mr. Davis, we are here today to question you about the book thefts from the WHI and your role in that."

"What are you talking about?"

"Sir, before you say anything else I must warn you that anything you say to us will be recorded and may be used in legal proceedings against you. You do not need to answer our questions but, if you do, you must tell the truth. You have the right to legal counsel before saying anything to us. Do you understand all of that?"

"Sure, sure. What are you saying about me?"

"Mr. Davis, we know that you have been stealing books from the WHI for over ten years. You have been supplying those books to organized criminals, including a certain Alberto Danza, who paid you for them. You started with the Thomas James publication years ago and finished with the Luke Foxe journal recently. You used the money that you received to go on extensive annual vacations, cruising in the Caribbean."

Dennis became incensed, almost unhinged, at hearing the FBI summarize his activities, actually his life, so simply and dispassionately. Totally disregarding the caution he had been given, he launched into a heated reply.

"Those books were being wasted here. No one comes to use them anymore. They just accumulate and stagnate as rich people donate them from their collections to get huge tax credits, all based on high market values that far exceed what they might have paid for them in the past. Those books should be going back to the market for people who actually appreciate them. Those guys at the Carnegie were doing the same thing: liberating hundreds of books."

The room fell silent, as Director Wright and the FBI agents absorbed what they had just heard. Not a denial, but a rationalization for large-scale theft.

Agent Wilson then quietly spoke up, hoping to prompt more information.

"So, you started all of that?"

"No, but when Alberto contacted me I soon became committed."

"For the money?"

"Of course, that too. Why should I be babysitting those books for low wages while others made large sums for just sticking them into oblivion?"

"Who else did you work with, other than Danza?"

"Just Alberto, no one else. I should have known something was going wrong when he didn't pay me for the Foxe. He just kept putting me off."

Agent Wilson was disappointed but not surprised. Sure, they essentially had a full confession from Dennis Davis, but they hadn't learned anything new.

"Mr. Davis, you are under arrest for conspiring and committing felonious grand theft."

75

The FBI agents gathered in a large meeting room the next morning. Additional help had been recruited due to the many tasks ahead of them. Well over fifty people were present.

Agent Wilson addressed the group.

"Thanks to everyone for being here on short notice. We are going to conduct a major series of arrests today and they need to be coordinated as closely together as we can manage. We want to avoid word of our actions getting ahead of us.

"Over the past decade or more there has been a concerted and coordinated theft of valuable books from major institutions in the region. This has amounted to over ten million dollars of theft. Along with that, there have been associated, extensive money laundering activities, again involving millions.

"The crimes have involved employees at the institutions who stole the books, many bookdealers who handled the books, and the criminal organization headed by Antonio Esposito, who masterminded and controlled the whole thing.

"Today we are going to arrest everyone that we know about in this vast conspiracy. Based on the evidence that we have gathered, court-approved arrest warrants have been issued.

"We will be regrouping into teams with specific tasks. As you entered the room today you were issued numbered tags, one, two or three.

"Twenty of you with the numbered-one cards should gather with Agents Ernie Haas and Karl Kolby at the back of the room. You will be raiding nine different bookdealers, arresting the managers and seizing their records.

"Ten of you with the numbered-two cards should meet with Agents Wilma Watkins and Leonard Nelson up front. You will be travelling to four of the institutions where the books were stolen. In one case you will be arresting an individual who was responsible for the thefts. In the other three cases, you will be involved in the briefing of the management at those places about the thefts and will hopefully await more information about possible arrests. We have technicians at work searching phone records that should identify the culprits.

Franklin's Fate

"The rest of you with numbered-three cards should join me and Agents Mark Barnett and Randy Stockton in the room next door. We will be coordinating the arrest of Tony Esposito and two of his associates. We will need a large group at each arrest for obvious reasons. They have been under careful surveillance since yesterday morning. We know where they are."

Epilogue

Epilogue

The wave of activity that followed was amazing. All of the planned arrests took place, with the exception of a couple of the first-line bookdealers who could not be located, as had happened with Second Reading Books earlier.

Media coverage was extensive. Agent Wilson had convened a press briefing for late in the day. The stories of major book thefts from large institutions and the involvement of the Esposito criminal organization dominated the headlines.

Court proceedings unfolded over many months.

The dealers from Go Forth and Read and Five Hills Books, who were located, were represented by their lawyers as being simple, hired employees, who had just provided data entry and basic internet services. They paid fines and were given suspended sentences with the requirement to undertake some community service activities.

Andrew Dunlop of CARBCo and the dealers at Book Clean Out and Clear the Attic Books were given somewhat larger fines and sentenced to eighteen months in jail, although they did not actually go to jail. They were placed on restricted movement conditions and reported to work programs for a year. Jails were too crowded and expensive for simple book manipulators.

Terrance Kent of Schuylkill River Books and his equivalent at Copper River Books did go to jail for two years and their assets were seized. They had processed millions of dollars of transactions and had not cooperated with the authorities in trying to locate where the stolen books had gone.

Francine Dumont and the people who had stolen the books from the other three institutions had also been given suspended sentences and assigned to community service projects. They had been represented as low-level participants who had been coerced by Alberto Danza. They had not actually received a lot of money, about $200,000 over ten years.

Dennis Davis was treated more severely. He was a senior member of the staff at WHI and had obviously been very involved and creative in his book thefts, as demonstrated by the elaborate scheme he had used to steal the Foxe. Nothing he told the FBI justified mitigating his case. He was sentenced to two years in prison.

The trial of Tony Esposito, Hugo Cici and Alberto Danza was a joint event focusing on the RICO conspiracy that overlay all of the other activities. They had good lawyers who challenged everything and used the terms conjecture, circumstantial and coincidence a lot. Nevertheless, they were convicted. The jury seemed to have an underlying outrage at the robbery of valuable books from public institutions. It seemed like a community pillage.

Alberto Danza, as the key organizer of the actual thefts and manipulator of the individuals involved, was sentenced to five years in prison.

Hugo Cici, as the overseer of the whole network of dealers and book manipulations, as well as the money laundering, and Tony Esposito, as the overall boss and strategic planner, were sentenced to ten years in prison.

Sasha Rusti's testimony had been critical in all those convictions.

Sasha Rusti was relocated to Seattle, Washington as a retired English professor from a small Midwest university. He easily disappeared into the large city. He disposed of the assets of Metro Rare Books over a period of time via the internet.

Agent Efrem Wilson and Director Sybil Stephens met in her office after the trials were complete.

"Well done, Agent Wilson. You perseverance and creativity paid off. Those criminals are in jail and the large-scale robbery of rare books has been stopped."

"Thank you. As I think back, I realize again how it usually takes some small mistake for criminals to be caught. They had been stealing those valuable books for many years without detection. Then a chain of events tripped them up.

"The lost Franklin ships are discovered in Canada. The thieves decide to concentrate on Arctic books. There is a Franklin Celebration in Ottawa that attracts the attention of the WHI. They discover some missing books and call us. Even after we are dead-ended, the baited trap that Herb Trawets suggested finally gave us the breakthrough. What if Rusti didn't go to Ottawa? If someone other than Sasha Rusti had been the one to present the Foxe to Trawets, we might never have uncovered the key to breaking the case, which was establishing his link to Esposito and getting him to testify."

"True, but you and your team did sort it all out."

"I wish we could have recovered more of the stolen books but they disappeared into the world of dealers and collectors. Just as with the books stolen from the Carnegie Library earlier, the books are not individually identifiable if they have been carefully cleaned up. The lack of sales destinations from Schuylkill River Books and Copper River Books left us with no direct leads. Obviously Cici and Esposito had decided that they would be more protected from discovery if the actual books could not be located and traced back to them."

"Right. Without any direct evidence, any dealer or collector who might wonder if a book they had came from the Carnegie or these later thefts has no incentive to present it. Identification would be difficult, and they could be out large sums of money."

"At least with the RICO convictions, the institutions can file civil suits with Esposito and his organizations to recover some value and to maybe acquire similar replacement books. They also have insurance."

"You know," said Director Stephens, "one other irony is that I had you initiate all of the investigations based on the sale of the fake book to President Cartwright and the disappearance of the millions of dollars. These people had nothing to do with any of that."

At varying times, Simon Katz, Margaret Thomas, Jeremy Boucher and others checked their records. Many of them had bought books over the years from Schuylkill River Books and Copper River Books.

As Simon says, "Who knows?"

Herb Trawets was again sitting on his patio, drink in hand, looking out at the sunset over the Pacific Ocean.

He had followed the news of the arrests and trials related to the book thefts with great interest. He hadn't had any more contact with the FBI. A nice note of thanks from Agent Wilson had been attached to the check he received in the mail for his consulting services.

He had enjoyed his involvement. He didn't have many exciting activities in his retirement.

His last thought was, "Yes, I must certainly destroy that last copy of the Sir Francis Drake document."

The End

Barry Stewart is a collector of antiquarian books and maps and avid reader of history related to the early exploration of northwest America and the Arctic. He divides his time between Alberta, British Columbia, and Arizona.

He has previously published *Across the Land...a Canadian journey of discovery*, which describes Canada's people, places, history, and idiosyncrasies, and *Drake's Dilemma* and *Vancouver's Vengeance*, the first books in this series that now includes *Franklin's Fate*.

If you would like to buy another copy of this book, you can contact Trafford Publishing via their bookstore at www.trafford.com or by phone at 1-888-232-4444. It is also available through major commercial websites such as Amazon, Chapters, or Barnes and Noble. Your local bookseller can certainly order it for you.

Printed in the United States
By Bookmasters